TILL DEATH US DEPART

ORDER OF THADDEUS

J. A. BOUMA

EmmausWay
PRESS

2:23 p.m.

The mainstay of the Western marriage vow tradition stretches all the way back to Thomas Cranmer—at least the Christian kind, particularly the non-Catholic kind. He was a leader of the Protestant Reformation, after all. I'd studied up on my marriage vow tradition in preparation for the big day.

My big day.

Because, if anyone could believe it, Silas Grey was getting hitched! And to the most amazingly beautiful, smartest, most capable, and loving woman on the planet.

Celeste Bourne.

We'd talked about writing our own vows, but I was never really any good at that sort of thing, expressing myself, my heart. I worried I'd forget my lines and mess things up, mess our day up.

So, Cranmer it was. All of it, too. The whole bit about taking her to be my wife, to have and to hold from this day forward. All of the *'for better for worse'* stuff—which was mostly for my sake; without that clause, I'd be a goner.

Same for the *'for richer for poorer, in sickness and in health.'* Neither of us had been rich, though we both had comfortable middle-class lives. And given our profession as the Church's special-ops agents, we were in good shape and good health. But nowadays, you never knew when the Big C would show its ugly face.

Was more than ready to pledge myself to *'love, cherish, and to obey'* Celeste—again, that last bit was for my own well-being!

Same for the final bit to the whole vow: pledging to fulfill all of the above *'till death us depart.'*

Just didn't expect to execute on that final clause so soon!

Because instead of saying my vows, I was running to take cover from—

A wicked *rat-a-tat-tat* sliced through the nave of the Washington National Cathedral, chewing through wood pews and sinking into limestone columns.

—that!

The strafing bullets, no doubt from some Heckler & Koch automatic rifle, the weapon of choice for a certain nemesis—sent me diving into the Children's Chapel and racing toward a slender, solid wood door.

Of course it was shut. Probably locked.

Which was pretty much par for the SEPIO course, the operational arm to the Order of Thaddeus, ancient defender of the Christian faith.

Was about the only option at this point.

Another livid set of relentless *rat-a-tat-tats* put an exclamation point on my current lot in life!

Leapfrogging over the back of the slender wood chairs, I landed with a sure footing on the crimson padded seats and dashed down the small aisle to sail back to the stone floor.

Catching the edge wrong and stumbling overboard.

Caught most of the impact with my right shoulder, but pain bloomed from my right knee and lanced up my leg.

I was getting too old for this...

I choked back a curse and hobbled for the door, grasping the burnished bronze knob and giving it a twist.

Moment of truth...

Unlocked.

A first for SEPIO!

Which did my heart good, but also sent all sorts of administrative signals pinging my Master of the Order brain. Should've been locked, a stairwell winding down below, but glad it wasn't.

Wasn't responsible for the facilities, but was sure glad

some janitor forgot to lockdown. A hefty bottle of Scotch whiskey with a big, red bow was in order for that blessed soul!

And a hefty raise.

Throwing opened the door, I dove inside and yanked it closed—

Just as another menacing barrage of bullets thudded with a useless muffle into the other side.

Without a clue where Celeste was.

Till death us depart, Cranmer had written.

Good words, holy words.

Just not for today.

Not this day.

The day I was supposed to get hitched.

———

11:03 a.m.

Today was the day I'd been waiting for—not necessarily my whole life, but certainly most of my life, given I thought I'd be consigned to eternal bachelorhood. The academy does that to you, as does the military, both of which had consumed my life for the better part of adulthood.

Heard once that Gandhi said God was the hardest taskmaster he'd ever known on this earth, trying you through and through. The Almighty had nothing on the academy and the Army!

Now the Church...that was a different story.

A relentless spouse, she could be! I'd been married to her official like going on three years now, the ring of betrothal having been passed along to me when Rowan Radcliffe passed, former Master of the Order of Thaddeus. He'd handed me the reins to one of the Church's premier religious orders contending for the faith, and quite unexpectedly, I might add. Had thought he would've handed them off to my bride-to-be. Frankly, so did everyone else in the Order, including the muckety-mucks on the board of directors. Might get their way yet if one of them had anything to say about it.

At any rate, taking Radcliffe's place as Master, a day didn't go by that I didn't have a honey-do list unfurled out the door taking care of the Church's housekeeping business! Most of it was your garden variety TPS reports keeping track of the Vatican's monthly allowance. Though the Order of Thaddeus was an ecumenical outfit, they still controlled the purse strings. Who knew? I sure didn't when I was brought on board.

Sure learned that lesson quick once we started edging into the red. Didn't help matters that my best man, Matt Gapinski, had an appetite for expensive foreign cars and, well, a massive appetite! Claimed it was because he was big-boned. I just think he had a third leg that was always hungry for another burger or glass of Balvenie whiskey.

Oh, wait, that was me.

Between balancing the books and defending the Good Book against assaults inside and outside the Church—compounded by gunfights and car chases and exploding drones, on top of a resurgent Knights Templar and government alien conspiracy...let's just say I had my hands full. That wasn't even touching on all the crazy brought on by the Church's nemesis stretching back to Christianity's founding—Nous, an ancient enemy that had risen from the shadows of history to rain down the wicked funk on the Church for the better part of half a decade after remaining dormant. Which I got embroiled in thanks to my own academic project proving the Shroud of Turin the authentic burial cloth of Jesus Christ —and thus proving his resurrection authentic.

Just my luck.

It was also my luck that said nemesis was headlined by my baby brother, Sebastian. That's a whole other story going back years—really since childhood, when an inciting incident (one among many that had made headlines the past few decades) sidetracked his faith and plunged him into a Cain-and-Abel fight with me, not to mention a Judas-and-Jesus betrayal with the good Lord above. Which I was caught in the middle of, and was tasked to keep at bay.

So, yeah. A honey-do list a mile long.

Could only imagine what was coming when I was actually married.

So my entire life waiting to marry, no. But definitely the last four years. Ever since I'd laid eyes on Celeste Bourne who was a Bourne before Bourne was a Bourne. Those chestnut locks, those striking azure eyes of hers, that polished Queen's English British had sent my heart soaring when we first met.

Probably helped that she saved my backside from no uncertain doom after a band of pseudo-spiritual whack jobs tried to kill me in a chapel at my alma mater! And then plenty more after that. But this was no White Knight Syndrome. Because, truth be told, I'd thought she was a bit snooty for her own good the first time we met. Seemed way to sure of herself, especially with the way she compared herself to that Robert Ludlum special-ops character.

Turned out, she had every right to be as cocksure as I thought she was!

Not only had she been Oxford educated, with graduate degrees in comparative religion and psychology. She'd also been plucked out from an elite unit within MI6 by Radcliffe to take charge of SEPIO, the special-ops arm of the Church tasked with assuming more kinetic endeavors.

The mission of the Order of Thaddeus had been at stake for generations. Jude was right: Christians needed to contend for the once-for-all-faith. To protect, instruct, fight for, watch over, heed what the Church had always believed. Which was everything that SEPIO was about, the muscular, special-forces arm of the Church she was responsible to lead.

Radcliffe had launched the project several decades ago, an acronym for *Sepio, Erudio, Pugno, Inviglio, Observo*—Latin for protect, instruct, fight for, watch over, heed. In a stroke of genius, he had recruited Celeste out of MI6 to lead its mission to preserve and protect the memory of the faith.

I'd joined a few years ago to preserve Christian objects and relics of the faith, as well as its memory and beliefs, surrounding the faith itself with a hedge of protection—mostly after I'd gotten sacked from Princeton, but I like to think the Holy Spirit had something to do with it.

For a while, Celeste was my boss, and for good reason. Roles reversed only when Radcliffe made me Master, but even then our success was in no small way due to her acumen and talent. She was way out of my league.

Yet, somehow she'd said yes—and waited for me to get my act together to finally plan our wedding and get hitched proper. Which was a whole thing in and of itself.

Started the night when our wedding planning at a nice French bistro in Dupont Circle, DC, was interrupted by an old flame from MI6, a spoke who'd brought us a crazy-ass case about a US government conspiracy involving Nazis and aliens. Par for the SEPIO course, but it turned out he was right. Put a massive crimp in our wedding plans, though, not to mention denied me a mean beef bourguignon I'd been hankering to eat for months.

If things couldn't get worse—which they always did in the story of my life—we had quite the trouble finding a minister to officiate. My childhood priest was murdered (not that I'd necessarily wanted him to officiate after what he'd done to my brother, but still; he'd also had a turnaround that absolved him of his past) and Celeste never had a family pastor. Her parents were more a freelance variety of Christianity, as she framed it. Whatever that meant I wasn't sure, given I was reared proper in as high church as you could go—with all the smells and bells and Latin liturgy and everything.

Thankfully, we were able to turn to an old friend, Peter Daniel Young. He'd helped us out of yet another SEPIO mess back in Michigan, when some charlatans were peddling deadly hope, and then again when our last operation brought us to a professor at a seminary a rogue government agency took out with a Black Hawk helicopter.

Again, par for the SEPIO course.

Thankfully, he'd agreed to officiate our wedding ceremony, and since the Order of Thaddeus was headquartered in the Washington National Cathedral, I was able to pull some strings to get us to hold our ceremony in one of the chapels as a last resort when our original venue fell through. Ironically, the very chapel that Rowen Radcliffe had asked me to join SEPIO as an operative to support the Order of Thaddeus.

Life has a way of coming full circle. And the Holy Spirit has a sense of humor, joining me to my new bride after he beckoned and wooed me to serve Christ's Bride as an agent protecting and preserving the faith.

So the day I'd been waiting for had finally arrived.

It was also the day I'd put off for far too long.

Had proposed to Celeste in a cemetery, of all things. I know, real romantic. Which made sense if you think about it, given she'd been kidnapped by my wackadoodle brother for some demonic ceremony sacrificing her to the spawn of Satan —well, more like for some demonic ceremony sacrificing her to the actual Satan!

Long story. One of many that had defined our relationship the past four years.

So after rescuing Celeste, I'd confessed my undying love for her. Going on about how she was the most intelligent, magnificent, kind-hearted, capable, and hottest woman I'd ever met in my life. Then, right there in the middle of a pagan altar stone, I'd popped the question: *'Celeste Bourne, will you marry me?'*

I'll never forget that look of hers.

At first, she took a breath, then her face fell. Before widening into a smile before she burst into tears and threw her arms around my neck. *'About bloomin' time!'* she'd said to me. Which I deserved. Had been way too casual about our relationship after it was clear to both of us we were into one another. Just thankful she said yes after I'd taken so long.

But then it took another—what, almost two years to get to it. Sometimes I can be a bit daft, in the parlance of Celeste's home country. Took a crazy alien government conspiracy interrupting our wedding planning to finally get my backside into high gear!

And there I was. Adjusting the black bow tie around my neck in a men's bathroom mirror down the hall from the sanctuary that would play host to our wedding. Struggling more like it! Never was any good at tying these sorts of things. Dad was perfect at it, the military colonel quite capable of dressing to the nines when it came to it.

Dad...

My heart sank at the sight of me in that mirror struggling with the tie, my own age lines sketching an image of my father over twenty years ago now, when he himself was in his midforties, like I was approaching. He'd gotten me settled into my dormitory at Georgetown University during the last week of a summer class I'd actually enjoyed. Trigonometry. Go figure. That was the last time I'd seen him. September 2001.

Because then a few days later, we'd gotten word of the first two planes just after class began. At first, we all thought it was a tragic mistake, the one plane plowing into the one tower in a way that seemed super tragic but also super random. Like someone forgot to address a faulty indicator light during the pre-flight rundown, leading to mechanical failure and a hella-crazy tragedy.

That theory went out the window when the second tower enveloped the second plane, that explosion of fire and glass on repeat for the rest of the day, smoke blooming from its wounded side. Right before the pair collapsed in a phantasmic show of fire and fury.

Classes got canceled, which wasn't the worst thing in the world. My classmates and I were told to retire to our dorms to watch and process and grieve.

Then it happened.

A distant rumble reminded me of the crash I'd sworn I'd heard echo all the way up the Potomac. Then a bloom of smoke was seen spinning up into the sky. A smoke signal, not warning of danger but marking death.

In my case, marking Dad's death.

It was the spark that lit the fuse of my life that had brought me to that moment standing in a bathroom a few stories under the National Cathedral. Signed up the minute I could to show those bastards back in Afghanistan who was boss, bleeding red, white, and blue all over that Army contract at the recruitment center. Was more than ready, willing, and able to avenge Dad's death right after graduating the next year.

Spent a few tours overseas, first in Afghanistan then ending in Iraq with the Army Rangers. Grad school at Harvard was next on the docket, studying religious studies with an emphasis in archaeology, eventually landing me a gig at Princeton University. That is until the Order came calling. Or rather, Nous came calling, trying to blow up my backside along with a chapel full of fellow relicologists who studied the Shroud of Turin. Would've succeeded, too, had Celeste not saved that backside!

Had been saving my backside ever since, which was why I

was standing in this bathroom trying to tie my tuxedo tie but failing miserably.

The good Lord above sure does work in mysterious ways.

Only wished Dad was still around to help me tie it! Had been working on the dang thing for half an hour and still couldn't get it right. Only had another half hour before I had to take my place to walk into my own personal happily ever after.

Best day of my life, aside from giving my life to Jesus Christ, to being adopted into his Church.

Bride one down, another to marry waiting in the wings.

If only I could tie this dang—

A rumbly muffle sounded from the hallway just outside the door.

Right before it swung open with a slamming *smack!*

"There you are!" Matt Gapinski crowed. "We've been looking all over for you!"

"Yeah, we thought you bailed," said Elijah Fox behind him.

I smirked. "Not on your life!"

"I can understand why." He whistled. "She wears white silk and lace well."

"Have you seen her?"

"Boy, have I ever! And boy, is Celeste a looker!"

Gapinski smacked the man's back. "She's also taken, pal. Or will be once our boy here finishes up crimping his hair, daubing on the makeup, and doing his nails!"

He held up his arm and tapped his wrist, my best man doing his best to keep me on track after a disastrous day had already left us two hours past schedule.

"What's keeping you?"

I held up the dang bow tie with two fingers, scrunching up my face.

He huffed a sigh. "What, your old man never taught you how to tie a tie?"

"Not one of these."

"So uncouth. Hand it over."

I did, and he got to work, slinging it around my neck—getting way too close for comfort, Gapinski and me nearly nose to nose with something rancid riding on his hot breath. A cross between sauerkraut and sautéed onions.

Could the day get any worse?

"Samir and Yusef here yet?" I asked, my foot tapping an irritated beat while Gapinski worked his bow-tie magic.

The pair, twin brothers, were buddies from way back in high school and then in college, us three playing sports together for the Falls Church Jaguars and then at Georgetown University. When 9/11 hit us our senior year in different ways—me losing Dad thanks to the terrorist whack jobs who'd plowed into his wing of the Pentagon; them two losing the country they'd only always known as Arab Americans thanks to terrorist whack jobs who made it hella hard for his family—all three of us signed up to fight Uncle Sam's war, managing to not only not get killed but stick it out together with the Army through our tours. When we were discharged, all three of us went on to grad school up the coast—me to Harvard, the twins to MIT. Kept in touch as life took us elsewhere, so it made total sense for them to stand up with me during the most important ceremony of my life apart from confirmation in the Church.

But they'd been delayed. Something about a fritz-out with their airline—and they were flying Delta! Was more of a United thing, and definitely an American Airlines thing. Celeste wanted to be safe flying everyone in on The World's Most Trusted Airline, as it was once known. They'd also claimed to be ready when you are—but apparently not today, of all days.

On my wedding day!

A harbinger of many more things-get-worse snafus in our

day. From our original venue, our home church in Arlington (busted pipe that flooded the sanctuary) to our reception hall (faulty wiring burned it down three days before).

So, of course my groomsmen were stranded on a plane!

Gapinski finished with my neck and frowned.

"Bupkis on the twin groomsmen front," he answered before grinning and slapping my shoulders. "But your tie is tied, your bride is ready to ride, and the show must go on. So let's saddle up, partner. *Yee haw!*"

I sucked in a breath and nodded, my stomach suddenly doing a cartwheel. More out of anticipation than nerves, but also out of disappointment. Just wanted the day to go right, to be right and be special. My groomsmen at my side as my radiant bride walked to me—to *me*, of all people! With the ceremony going off without a hitch and Peter Young sending us off into marital bliss to eat and drink and dance the afternoon away as we launched Day One of the rest of our lives. Together, as one.

Till death us depart.

The door swung open again, and in popped another familiar face.

Peter Young, looking all dapper in his heather gray suit matching my groomsman and sporting the deep purple necktie that Gapinski and Eli wore, matching Celeste's bridesmaids' dresses.

Grinning, he approached and extended a hand. "There he is, the man of the hour!"

I shook it, heaving a shaking breath and smiling. "It's go time.

"And on the double. I've been told to get you into position. You ready to get to it?"

Another breath with a nod. "Let's get this party started!"

"Yeah, buddy," Gapinski said. "Now that's what I'm talking about!"

12:01 p.m.

There was still another hour or so until the ceremony started. Celeste was still holed up in her own room getting primped and prepped. Hadn't seen her yet. Couldn't wait to see her!

Couldn't wait for that moment when she came down the aisle to get my first glimpse of her in all her radiance—her long, wavy chestnut hair she'd been growing out for the wedding all done up; that white, lacy silk dress of hers with the train that stretched several yards behind; her beautiful face accented just right by makeup she didn't need but loved wearing.

Again, couldn't wait to see her!

Heat raced up my neck thinking about that moment when I saw my bride face-to-face. Sort of reminded me of the way Scripture speaks of Christ meeting his own Bride, the Church, on the day of our own Wedding Feast when he returns to gather his followers to himself for all eternity.

No till death us depart in that marriage!

Speaking of which...

I'd slipped up a set of stone stairs to the surface level to get some air, coming out into the narthex of the Cathedral Church of Saint Peter and Saint Paul—better known as the Washington National Cathedral, where the Order's headquarters was stationed down below. While it was sort of a default national church, hosting plenty of funerals for American dignitaries, it was also a working church, the massive nave hosting weekly Sunday services.

My escape was a welcomed relief after being holed up in the belly of the cathedral since the morning waiting for the ceremony to unfold—waiting for my life to unfold. Nothing had gone right, and I was waiting for things to get worse on what should have been the best day of my life.

By now it was high-noon, with the early summer sunlight fighting for a hearing through storm clouds emerging from the west. Not enough to dampen the day—yet, but it was worrisome. I'd always been a firm believer in the sailor's warnings about those things. Had woken to an inflamed horizon, the red sky signaling no uncertain doom ahead, which had been confirmed in more operations than I cared to count.

Fortunately, for now, the billowing stacks of charcoal had nothing on the high-noon, its light cascading orange and warm through the three porticos facing southwest. It was bright; it was hot—not stifling, just nice against the face. A hot breath of summer gusted from the south now, a whipping wind carrying with it the last vestiges of the cherry blossom trees that had faded from spring, the air soft and silky and sweet.

But I couldn't enjoy any of it. Too anxious, too ready to get to it. It was go time—it *had* been go time.

So I paced the nave and kept an eye on the sky, the smell of old stone and wood, tinged by a bit of that wet basement from Falls Church childhoods, joined by the pulp and metalicy tang of copier paper settling me, grounding me.

Guests were milling about outside—checking watches, killing time, coming in and out through the tall, wide entrance doors.

Felt a twinge of regret for how their day had been messed up by our delays. But I couldn't do anything about that now. And frankly, I couldn't care. Had to keep my head in the game, in the mission—which was to get hitched. Me and Celeste.

If it was the last thing I did.

Spent the next half an hour playing host, roaming from huddled group to couples inside the nave and outside on the front cathedral lawn, those clouds becoming definite storm clouds now. Which would put a definite damper on our day of bliss. By now we should've been hitched and finished our wedding photos. Instead, my face and hands hurt from smiling and shaking hands, all the while I kept looking over my shoulder for Gapinski, for Naomi Torres, one of SEPIO's finest operatives and Celeste's maid of honor—anyone who would come rushing to tell me we were good to go.

Bupkis on that front.

So I did what anyone would do. I sought out the Four Evangelists for solitude.

Yes, that's right. Matthew, Mark, Luke, and John.

No, not in the Holy Scriptures. Their relics. An exhibit I had personally curated. What else is the Master of the Order of Thaddeus to do than live out his Indiana Jones wish-fulfillment dreams?

Not that I had to go hunting them down or anything like our intrepid fedora-wearing hero. Just made some calls to an old friend with the Vatican Archives.

Yes, those Vatican Archives!

Had wanted to bring the bearers of the Good News of Jesus Christ together for sometime, fascinated by not only their witness to Jesus' life, death, and resurrection, but also their martyrdom for the sake of that witness. Their historical biographies chronicling Jesus' life, death, and resurrection had not only carried me through my tours overseas in the Middle East for Uncle Sam. They'd also sustained and nourished my faith in those early years after fully committing my life to Christ.

So, to be able to secure their memory markers, to bring them together in an organized exhibit that let others experience the magic of their witness to what Jesus had taught and how he had lived, to his payment for our sins in our place on those boards of execution and his defeat of death through the resurrection—it was a dream come true!

First, there was Saint Matthew, his Gospel written to Jewish Christians to connect the Jesus Story to their Jewish Story, mapping out his fulfillment of their expectations for the coming Messiah. Although the manner of his death was uncertain, it was believed he was martyred, and his bones enshrined in Salerno, Italy.

Next up was Mark, the shortest of the Four, but also thought to be the primary source for the others—at least Matthew and Luke. He was also thought to be an African, from the North, who accompanied Saint Paul on his missionary journeys. Although his relics had remained in Alexandria for some time, Venetian merchants had purchased them, where a grand basilica shrine was erected.

Then Luke, who I had personally taken to, the man approaching Jesus' story as a historian, like myself. As a physician, there was a precision and method to Luke's investigation of the claims surrounding Jesus—his miracles and teachings, his death and resurrection—that I found compelling. While he must have suffered much for the faith, especially given his journeys in the Book of Acts, it's unclear how he died. His relic bones had been disputed, between two territories, Padua and Venice, with the former winning out.

Finally, John, who was unlike all the others. His stated goal in the twentieth chapter of his Gospel was to write his account *'so that you may continue to believe that Jesus is the Messiah, the Son of God, and that through believing you may have life in his name.'* He was also the author of the Apocalypse, the revelatory account of the end of the world as we know it. Tradition holds he was boiled in a vat of oil during the Domitian persecution, and then sent to the Island of Patmos where he experienced his apocalyptic revelation. Surviving, he moved to Ephesus, where he served as bishop before his death. A shrine marked his ministry, but a basilica in Turkey marked his death.

And there they were. In all their final glory.

The displays were set up just inside the reception threshold area to the massive nave that stretched a football field. Glass cases gleamed along the back limestone wall soaring toward the buttresses, massive stained glass windows dappling the main sanctuary stretching toward the altar in ruby and amber, sapphire and topaz, emerald and golden citrine. Although, their light was fading with each passing quarter hour, the sky darkening and dimming the sunlight.

The clacking of my stiff black patent oxford shoes echoed around me as I approached the displays, whispered conversations and scuffing chairs thrown up across the sacred space around me. Only portions of the entire collection of each martyrs bones were included: a femur from Saint Luke's leg, a metacarpal from Saint Matthew's right hand, part of Saint John's skull, and Saint Mark's mandible. Each sat in ornately decorated gold reliquary boxes befitting the Evangelists, the bone relics resting upon crimson pillows and glistening white under overhead lighting in all their sacred radiance within secure polycarbonate glass cases.

I stood still, crossing my arms and taking in a contemplative breath, the world outside fading away for a moment.

An older couple edged my way, interrupting me from my contemplation, from my moment of breathing. Introduced themselves in a very posh English accent, so definitely from the bride's side of the aisle. Friends of the family, they were, who had seen my picture from the social media WeShare site. I directed them downstairs, but then others queued up, introducing themselves as well—mostly from Celeste's side, but also some of my own family and friends.

Apparently, boredom had set in real good, and they were eager to pass the time.

A trio of men in tuxedos were eyeing the collection of the Apostle John. Figured I should play host and introduce myself. Didn't want to in the slightest, my cheeks hurting now from all the glad-handing. But I walked over anyway.

Looked Persian on a second assessment. Not Iraqi or Jewish. Maybe Saudi or Iranian? Wouldn't surprise me in the slightest where they were from, given Celeste's globetrotting adventures with MI6 and her multicultural leanings. Much more cosmopolitan than me!

Clearing my throat, I offered, "Quite the exhibit, isn't it?"

The tall, broad-shouldered middle man glanced over, offering a slight nod, neither of his wingmen offering the same. All lookalikes, actually. Angular facial features, dark eyes, dark hair cut close to the sides and coiffed on top. Definitely government-issued. And definitely must be from Celeste's days in the Secret Intelligence Service, commonly known as MI6.

"The groom, I presume?" the middle man said, a polished Queen's English lilt to him, like Celeste, giving me a once-over before smiling and turning my way.

I nodded with a chuckle. "I'd be the one."

The trio pivoted toward me, tattoos peeking from behind their collars now as their suits shifted along with them.

"And your *exhibit*, I presume—" Middle Man leaned in "—Master Grey."

I could feel my cheeks warm at the recognition.

"That's right. And you are...."

"Ah," he said clutching a hand to his chest, "where are my manners. Hamid Assan." He outstretched his hand.

I took it, a hard hand that had seen action. Definitely not desk-work hands.

"And since I don't know you," I said, pulling back and shoving my hands in my pockets, "I presume you're here for the better half of the aisle?"

Assan chuckled, glancing at his companions. "We know one another from her service with MI6."

"Ah. That makes sense. She got around."

He smiled and dipped his head. "That she did."

The seconds ticked by, us four standing next to the four Evangelists as a few guests meandered around us. I went to check my watch, eager for a look-see at the time, when—

"Tell me," Assan said, gesturing at the cases, "you've managed to assemble all of the Evangelist relics. I have been an admirer for some time and would count it a holy act to be able to venerate them whilst I memorialize your and Celeste's marriage."

I narrowed my eyes, catching a tinge at the back of my lizard brain throwing up a—something. Didn't know what; didn't make sense, not in the slightest.

But I nodded. "That's right. My connections with the Vatican Archives allowed me to—"

"Silas!" a voice echoed from the front of the nave, interrupting me.

All four of our heads snapped toward the interruption.

Now it boomed: "Paging Doc Grey. Here, Silas Silas Silas."

Matt Gapinski.

The lug was lumbering from one of the side chapels, apparently having surfaced through one of the narrow stairwells—and still calling my name!

I chuckled, heat racing up my neck in embarrassment. "Excuse me, I should—"

Didn't bother finishing, instead skimming across the stone floor as fast as my aching feet would take me in those stiff oxfords.

"Gapinski!" I said in a whispered rush, waving my arms, the soaring limestone columns carrying my voice with an echo.

He snapped his head toward my racing self and threw up a cat-call holler.

"The man of the hour himself!"

Heads turned, giggles were thrown up, people shuffled our way for news.

My whole body burned with the heat of embarrassment now at the show, compounded by my hustling feet and throbbing heart.

"Keep it down, would you?" I hissed with more vinegar than I intended. "Is there word?"

"You bet your sweet bippy there's word!" Gapinski exclaimed with far too much volume. Didn't bother with a correction, because his wide face and bright eyes told me all I needed to know.

"So, she's ready?"

"More than ready. She's in place!"

"What?" I exclaimed, echoing far too loudly. Didn't care.

If Celeste was in place, that meant I was out of place.

Which meant I was late!

Story of my life.

"Why didn't you get me!" I hissed again, racing a trembling hand through my hair, more from excitement now than from nerves.

Gapinski frowned. "Uh, I just did…"

Went to retort but left it alone. Man had a point.

Instead, I heaved a stabilizing breath and nodded with a grin.

"It's go time, then?"

He slapped me on the back. "On the double, solider."

"Where do I—"

A shrilly *bring-bring-bring* cut me off, high and heady and sounding alarm.

An actual alarm, the one keeping the Evangelists safe and secure!

A rumble of startled cries and confusion from a huddled group at the nave's entrance joined the bleating alarm. Not what I needed on my wedding day, not in the slightest. But duty called. For a few minutes I wasn't Silas the Groom but Silas the Order Master.

I jogged down the long center aisle, my clacking shoes drowned by the shrieking *bring-bring-bring*. Gently pushing through the crowd of onlookers, I found the friends-of-the-family British couple standing stiff, like the proverbial deer in headlights. They looked positively mortified at the faux pax.

Finding the alarm keypad, I quickly typed in the disarming code.

Eliciting another bout of shrilly *bring-bring-brings!*

"Sonofa—" Gapinski cursed behind. "What the heck is wrong with that thing?"

Clenching my jaw, I jammed in the code again.

Still nothing but sirens. Which would bring real sirens if I didn't get this blasted thing shut down!

Could things get any worse?

"Are you kidding me..." I growled, punching in the code again—my birthday! "Why isn't this—"

Then it hit me.

And I laughed out loud, the alarm roiling into a panic now.

"Laugh it up, fuzzball," Gapinski complained. "What's so funny?"

I pecked at the keypad one more time, inputting the right set of numbers this time.

The echoey shrill finally wound down to zero. I sighed a breath I didn't know I was holding.

"Finally!" Gapinski offered me his hand. "What did the trick?"

I took it, hoisting myself back to my feet. "Simple. Celeste's birthday."

"She always was the one who saved the day."

"Don't I know it!"

The poor elder couple were positively mortified, but I reassured them all was fine.

Gapinski grabbed my elbow and started gently leading me away. Like he said earlier: Time to go, on the double.

I announced the impending festivities—to much fanfare—and led the charge navigating the crowd back down to the chapel beneath the cathedral.

The stage was set, so we began.

A steady hum permeated the dimly lit, modest Indiana limestone Bethlehem Chapel a floor beneath the National Cathedral, filling the sacred space with a sense of sacred significance. The hum of voices and whispered conversations, the hum of gathered family and friends shuffling about to finally take their seats in polished oak pews.

Recessed lighting offered a dim orange glow, while little flames danced on four long candles near a solid white limestone altar. It sat in front of an intricate limestone facade of miniature statues of the four Gospel writers, behind oak altar rails with kneeling cushions patterned in red and gold. Beautiful stained-glass windows depicting biblical scenes in crimson red and leafy green, gold yellow and indigo blue, normally blazing bright with awe-inspiring light, were kept in dim darkness from the coming storm spitting against their glass outside now.

The site was set to play host to a sacred rite.

The sacrament of holy matrimony.

The room was filled with family from both sides, with friends and colleagues from across the years and continents, new and old.

Missing were my family. A smattering of aunts and uncles had come to celebrate the special day, but the ones who mattered most were missing.

Dad. Sebastian, who in a different life would've stood with me as a groomsman; that ship had long sailed.

Mom...

A twinge of regret wound through my belly. Never knew my mother. She'd passed giving birth to me and Sebastian, my twin. Hardly ever thought of her in all my years. Last time was baking and sweating under a mid-July sun at one end of Arlington National Cemetery burying Dad. But now, in that moment...

Sometimes a man needs his mama. Especially on his wedding day.

Instead, I took satisfaction in walking Penny Bourne to the front, my future mother-in-law.

Then I took one last trip, this time with Peter, the pair of us walking down to the front to get things started. With me and my groomsmen pair, Gapinski and Elijah Fox, along with Celeste's bridesmaids waiting for her arrival—Naomi Torres, looking as radiant as ever, even without her hair from recent chemo treatments, and Zoe Corbino, our SEPIO techie in her bright blue oversized glasses, joined by some of Celestes's mates.

We were all there, ready to go.

It was go time.

On the double.

Which was suddenly signaled by the organ changing its timber and tone, shifting its pitch and direction announcing the moment I had been waiting for.

The moment my bride arrived!

Pachelbel's "Canon in D" was the clarion call that brought the room to its feet.

The echoey shuffle quickly silenced down to nothing when a woman in white, joined by her father in black, appeared at the threshold to the chapel.

There she was. Celeste Ann Bourne, standing in all of her brilliance and radiance. Hair swept up into a glorious hive, festooned with small, white flowers of some kind. Dress white and lacy and billowy, trailing behind and shimmering in the candlelight. Face accented by the slightest touch of makeup, highlighting her cheekbones and luscious lips and sparkling eyes. Eyes that were glistening with tear-filled joy and a mouth that was the widest I'd seen, not only on Celeste but on any person.

The sight was pure magic. I'll never forget it as long as I live.

And now she was inching down the aisle paved in rose petals, an arm slung inside the crook of her father Paul's arm, heading my way.

Heading to me!

Lord Jesus Christ, Son of God, what on earth did I do to deserve such grace—such a gift?

The closer she came, the more enraptured I was. Yes, cliché, but my breath was stolen, literally my burning lungs a reminder to heave a stabilizing breath before I keeled over. Thought my heart would explode from my chest it was so full of exuberance and dumbfounded disbelief it was happening —to me!

It was so full of love, a love I can't recall feeling until that one night in a military chapel way back when in Iraq, when I pledged my life to my Savior, Jesus Christ, receiving his gift of salvation. I'd become part of the Bride of Christ that day, the Church, having served her in my capacity as Order Master. A Bride that certainly had its faults but was beautiful in its own, quirky sort of way.

Not gonna lie, but the Bride of Christ had nothing on Celeste!

Our eyes locked, and whatever breath was left in my lungs suddenly escaped to nothing but nothing. My head felt faint, eyes started sparking with starlight, knees started going wobbly—

And that's when I heaved a stabilizing breath, keeping my

eyes locked on Celeste, her gaze the Death Star's tractor beam. But in a good way!

Before I knew it, she was standing a few feet away with her dad. Like I'd been in some time warp or something, the seconds snapping together in an instant.

Pachelbel's magisterial music wound down to its finalizing note, signaling the beginning of the end to my black-and-white life, and the start to a brand-spanking new one full of high-definition color.

About damn time!

Celeste threw me a wink, her mouth holding her elated grin.

Thought I'd melt then and there. Almost did, my knees going wobbly again!

But I held it together, snapped back to the moment by Pastor Young.

Peter motioned with his hands, flattening his palms and waving them down.

"Please be seated," he said.

The audience obeyed, the small chapel filling with the shuffle of feet and groans of wood pews.

Smiling and lifting his hands, he went on, "I want to welcome you to this beautiful day. Yes, it's rainy, but it is still a gorgeous day because two people have heard the call of God on their lives to become one through the holy sacrament of marriage and are stepping out in obedience to that call."

An agreeing murmur swept through the witnesses, while a jitter swept through my nerves, coiling in my belly.

This was getting real.

"As a community 'tif friends and family," Peter continued, "we are gathered here in God's presence to witness two stories becoming one. This bond and covenant of marriage was established by God in creation, and our Lord Jesus Christ adorned this manner of life by his presence and first miracle at the wedding in Cana in Galilee. Marriage signifies to us the mystery of the union between Christ and the Church, and the Holy Scriptures commends it to be honored among all people."

Glancing into the audience, I caught nods and a few Amens.

"The union of husband and wife in heart, body, and mind is intended by God for their mutual joy; for the help and comfort given one another in times of abundance and scarcity; and when it is God's will, for the birth of children and their nurture in the knowledge and love of the Lord. Therefore, marriage is not to be entered into rashly or lightly—but reverently and deliberately, and in accordance with the purposes for which it was instituted by God."

Taking a breath, Peter gestured toward me and then to Celeste still standing with her father a few paces in front.

"Today, we gather to witness the marriage of Silas Grey and Celeste Bourne and ask God to bless them in their new union. They have heard the call of God upon their lives and are seeking to obey him by coming here together to be joined in marriage. And we are called as their community to rejoice in their happiness, to help them when they have trouble, and to remember them in our prayers. Jesus said when a man and woman come together in marriage they are no longer two, but one flesh. Out of two stories comes one new one. Out of two lives comes one new life. Therefore, what God has joined together, let no one separate."

Peter folded his hands in front of him and fixed his gaze at Celeste and her father.

"Who gives this woman to be married to this man?"

Emotion suddenly gripped Paul Bourne's face, his eyes misting over and cheeks reddening before a tremor took control of his lower lip.

Swallowing, then clearing his throat, he managed, "Her mother and I."

The two embraced, my almost-father-in-law giving his daughter a peck on each cheek before sending her on her way.

To me!

My breath caught again at her approach. When I regained it, heaving a lungful of air, my senses swam in lavender and vanilla. The smell of Celeste.

Did nothing for my heart, my ticker galloping even faster now at her closeness, at our almost-matrimony. But it did settle my jumble of nerves, her scent, her presence.

Simply her...

"Hey there, hot stuff," she whispered to me, leaning in against my shoulder as we turned toward Pastor Young.

I suppressed a chuckle, managing a "Hey there, yourself" before the wheels of ceremony clicked into place.

"We acknowledge openly," Peter continued, "that it is by God's kindness and plan that we live at all. It is by God's love that we are redeemed, and by God's providence that you have been brought together for this moment and for life. It is appropriate, therefore, that we pause to pray."

I closed my eyes, leaving one eye open to peek.

Catching Celeste doing the same!

Our eyes met, snatching my breath from me again.

"Father in Heaven," Peter intoned, snapping my eyes shut, "thank you for the gift of life, for family and friends, and for the love that exists between Silas and Celeste. As we assemble here together in the name of Jesus Christ, we are mindful of the guidance of your Spirit, who has brought us to this event, and mindful of the continuing need for your Spirit's help if the intentions declared this day are to be fulfilled. We turn, therefore, to you and in faith ask not only that you will be a part of this wedding ceremony, but also that you will enhance the lives of these your servants in this their union. Our God, we commit to you the very sacred moments that follow, praying your blessing and love would guide Silas and Celeste for years to come, through Jesus Christ. Amen."

The entire room echoed with an agreeing *Amen*.

I managed one myself, crossing myself on instinct.

"Silas and Celeste," Peter went on, "in just a few minutes you will seek to publicly acknowledge the purpose of God for your marriage and you will declare your mutual commitment to each other and to these goals. I want you to know fully what your choice of Christian marriage means for you."

As Pastor Young went on, Celeste grabbed my hand and squeezed it.

Not once, not twice.

Three times.

Our code.

For: *I. Love. You!*

A tingle raced through my arm, skating through my shoulder and up my neck into my face. Throat grew thick with emotion and eyes misted over from the fact of the matter.

Almost forgot to return the Morse code getting caught up in it all. Paid not a lick of attention to whatever Peter was going on about. Probably good stuff, too. Stuff I should listen to, pay heed. Nope, nothing doing! Not with anticipation racing through me.

I did manage to pull myself together enough to offer *a one-two-three-four* squeeze.

I. Love. You. Tooooo!

"I invite you," Peter said, snapping me back to the moment, "and all of us to listen to the words of the apostle Paul in his first letter to the Church at Corinth. In chapter 13, you are reminded of the kind of love that you are called to have for each other."

He opened his Bible and read:

Suppose I speak in the languages of human beings or of angels. If I don't have love, I am only a loud gong or a noisy cymbal. Suppose I have the gift of prophecy. Suppose I can understand all the secret things of God and know everything about him. And suppose I have enough faith to move mountains. If I don't have love, I am nothing at all. Suppose I give everything I have to poor people. And suppose I give myself over to a difficult life so I can brag. If I don't have love, I get nothing at all.

Love is patient. Love is kind. It does not want what belongs to others. It does not brag. It is not proud. It does not dishonor other people. It does not look out for its own interests. It does not easily become angry. It does not keep track of other people's wrongs. Love is not happy with evil. But it is full of joy when the truth is spoken. It always protects. It always trusts. It always hopes. It never gives up.

Love never fails. But prophecy will pass away. Speaking in languages that had not been known before will end. And knowledge will pass away.

A GOOD WORD from the Good Book, that's for sure! Would have to return to those verses once we got back from our honeymoon. Had a feeling I'd need them once we got into the swing of—

A moan, followed by a rumbly thud, with an added *chunka-chunka-chunka* was thrown up from my right.

Joined by a muttering curse and a smattering of gasps from behind. Along with an "Oh my cheeps!" from Elijah Fox.

If the sounds weren't enough, Peter's said it all. Pained and panicked.

I spun toward the commotion.

Finding Gapinski had flat fainted, my best man big-boned bruiser having fallen back into Eli before slumping into the empty first row and slid to the floor in a heaping pile of tuxedo and Gapinski, with Elijah pinned underneath.

"Get him off of me!" he complained, one of the latest additions to the crew as director of Group X. Knew the man wasn't fond of physical touch and tight spaces, given his neural uniqueness on the autism spectrum.

"Get him off of me! *Get him off of me!*" he complained louder. His partner, Gina Anderson, was at his side now, consoling him and yanking at his arm, but it was no use. Gapinski had him pinned to the ground something fierce. And Eli was becoming fiercer over the pinning by the second.

Not what he had in mind for his wedding day!

Naomi Torres got to the pair first, darting from behind to Gapinski's side. Figured, since they were partners, joined at the hip on most missions. And she didn't waste any time getting him to come to.

Slap! her palm sounded, sharp and insistent.

Then again: *Slap!*

This time with the back of her hand.

Went for round three when Gapinski snorted back to the land of the living.

I knelt beside him, Celeste at my side and Peter hovering over my back. Several in the audience had risen to their feet as well, gawking at the sorry scene.

"My head hurts..." he moaned, a meaty palm rubbing the back of his head. Torres and I helped him ease upright. "What'd I miss?"

"You fainted, *muchacho*," she said. "That's what you missed!"

"Low blood sugar. I'm famished. Thought we'd be eating by now."

Celeste mumbled, "Of course it was your hunger that led to our wedding misadventure."

Torres snorted a laugh. "Suppose it wouldn't be a SEPIO operation without Gapinski's stomach getting in the way."

"Can somebody get him off of me?" Elijah complained loudly again.

She and I completed our helping hand, hooking a hand under his arms to help him stand, Elijah scrambling out from underneath.

"Here, mate, drink this." Celeste handed him a glass of water kept at the altar for Peter.

Gapinski took a sip, then another, sighing and nodding his thanks. Poor guy was whiter than his tube socks, and a sweaty sheen reflected in the dim lights across his face.

"We good?" Peter asked after a minute.

Gapinski swallowed and nodded, taking a deep breath and motioning for him to get on with it.

Peter nodded, returning to his Bible and taking out a piece of paper. His notes, I assumed.

Rubbing his forehead, he threw on his best the-show-must-go-on smile and dove into the final lap of the ceremony.

At least I hoped it was!

We all filed back into place, Celeste and me front and center, with Gapinski looking wobbly to my right but standing strong along with Elijah, then with Torres back at Celeste's side and the other bridesmaids.

Heaving a breath, Peter began: "Silas and Celeste, I have a question for you: What is love?"

He let the question hang, Celeste throwing me a glance and a grin.

"Is it a *feeling*—those butterflies that fluttered away inside your belly, Silas, when you first met Celeste?"

"Ha!" she said. "Fat chance of that. Didn't have time after I rescued his ass."

The room erupted in laughter, a good tension valve after the way the day had gone.

I laughed. "That about summarizes how our relationship began."

Which brought on more laughter—and very much welcomed!

"Alrighty then," Peter said, chuckling. "Don't know what to do with that, so I'll move it along."

"Good call," Celeste said.

"What she said!" I replied.

More laughter before Peter continued with his prepared words: "Is it a *word*? 'I love you' are the three most common words uttered I'd imagine. Or is it an *act*? Celeste cooking—"

Now it was my turn: "Ha! Fat chance of that. I do all the cooking!"

Which sent the chapel roaring to new heights.

And Celeste sending a well-aimed fist into my shoulder. "I'd watch your Ps and Qs if I were you," she said, one end of her mouth curling upward.

Roiling the room into an even saucier boil than they'd been.

"Yes, dear..."

"Better rehearse those two words from here to Sunday..." Gapinski muttered. "Because that cat packs a punch!"

Right on the money he was!

Peter laughed now. "Not sure I can salvage this wedding sermon after all that, but I'll try!"

Which kept up the levity.

The room died down, and Pastor Young got back to it: "So, what is love? Well, one of Jesus' disciples, John, wrote a letter to some Christians and gave us our answer. He said in his first letter, chapter 3, *'This is how we know what love is: Jesus Christ laid down his life for us. And we ought to lay down our lives for each other.'*"

An apt description, one that sent my ears paying closer attention.

"What is love? Jesus Christ, Son of God, laying down his life on the cross—dying a bloody, painful death. For your sins, for my sins, for the world's sins. *That's* what love is. The Apostle Paul spoke of this love in a letter to the Church at Philippi. Listen to what he wrote about this kind of love—a love that Jesus Christ offers not only as a model for how we should live with each other, but also as the perfect blueprint for how a husband and wife should live with one another."

Clearing his throat, he read:

In his very nature he was God.

Jesus was equal with God. But Jesus didn't take advantage of that fact.

Instead, he made himself nothing.

He did this by taking on the nature of a servant.

He was made just like human beings.

He appeared as a man.

He was humble and obeyed God completely.

He did this even though it led to his death.

Even worse, he died on a cross!

Peter closed his Bible and eyed Celeste, then me.

"Jesus left behind any right to any special treatment. There was no pride in this selfless suffering servant. We are so quick to demand our own way and rights. Not Jesus. He made himself nothing. He willingly became a servant. And as a selfless, humble servant, Jesus suffered and died for both of you and for all of us here today."

Taking a breath, then a beat, Peter landed the plane.

"That is what should guide your love for each other. The

love you share together is only made possible because of God's love for you and for every person on the planet. And Paul urges us—urges *you* as followers of Jesus and as married people—to live in a way that's worthy of the cross, no matter what happens in your new life. Jesus laid down his life for each of you, and Paul urges you to lay down your life for each other as a servant just like Jesus. Every. Single Day. And now, here's your opportunity to promise to do that."

Peter motioned with his hands for us to turn toward one another.

Here we go. The vows.

I heaved a breath—

Just as the power cut to nothing but the flickering candle flames at the altar.

"Uhh..." Gapinski said, "did someone forget to pay the power bill, chief?"

I huffed a sigh. Could things get any worse?

A bassy rumble spread through the ceiling above now.

Apparently they could!

————

1:27 p.m.

My legs went wobbly with a trembling that bloomed then dialed down to nothing. But not before toppling over a lit candlestick, the orange flickering flame snuffing out to a thin strand of weaving smoke. Dust and flicking plaster fell from the ceiling, and a hairline crack opened up down the center.

Confirming a dreadful conclusion the second those lights cut to nothing but nothing.

"What the bloody hell was that?" Celeste muttered, glancing at the ceiling.

I turned to her, clenching my jaw and easing in a steadying

breath. Good question. Only one answer in my mind.

"Earthquake?" Gapinski said.

Torres slugged Gapinski; he yelped. "That was no earthquake, *muchacho!* That was some sort of *detonación.*"

"Detonation?"

"*Sí, detonación.*"

"Detonation?" Peter asked on a shaky breath.

"Is there an echo in here?" Elijah quipped.

Torres was right, though. Had heard more than my fair share of bomb blasts to last a lifetime thanks to Uncle Sam and his overseas misadventures. So I'd recognize the bassy reverberations and tremors of an explosive eruption. Whether up close and personal or a quarter mile away—even a few stories underground.

And this was that.

Some sort of detonation.

But a blast at the National Cathedral—

On my wedding day?

Peter turned to me, saying lowly. "You think this was some sort of bomb, Silas?"

Guests were murmuring now, glancing at one another in rushed, panicked whispers. Some were moving into the aisles

Celeste came up to us. "I suppose some electrical station could have given way, or a gas main bursting up above."

"Come on guys," Gapinski snorted, his vim and vigor having returned. "Is it any question?"

"*No, no es una pregunta,*" Torres said.

"She's right," I said. "It's not a question. This has Nous written all over it."

"And me without my trusty Sig Sauer," Gapinski cursed.

"So much for your first rule of the SEPIO road."

"Yeah yeah yeah. Never leave home without cold, hard steel. But we're at HQ, chief. And your wedding, for Pete's sake!"

"Here, take mine." It was Elijah, handing over his Glock.

"And mine," Gina Anderson said, joining the team from the restless audience.

Gapinski said, "Dude, you were packing at Silas's wedding?"

"Uh, yeah…" Eli replied, as if the question was as ridiculous as asking the color of the sky.

"Looks like the new guy's shown us seasoned SEPIO veterans up."

Celeste cleared her throat, nodding toward Gina.

"And new gal."

"Good lad." She retrieved Gina's weapon; I followed her lead by taking Elijah's. "But what's the design? What's the point?"

I shook my head, chambering a round and looking over the weapon.

Wasn't my weapon of choice. Much more preferred the Beretta Army-issued sidearm that had gotten me through a few tours of duty with Uncle Sam. But supposed it would do the job. And if it was good enough for the FBI, I supposed it was good enough for—

A thought suddenly struck me.

The alarm. The men.

"The Evangelists…"

"What's that love?" Celeste asked.

I turned to her. "The relic exhibit, in the main nave of the National Cathedral above."

"Of Matthew, Mark, Luke, and John?"

"Right."

"What of it?"

"There was a—mishap."

She raised an eyebrow. "A mishap."

"Oh, yeah," Gapinski added. "Those old folks messing with the glass cases setting off that redonk alarm."

"What old folks?"

"He's right," I replied. "There was an older couple who appeared to have triggered the alarm. But now...I'm not so sure it was them."

"Who then?" Gapinski asked.

"The ones who are hell bent on destroying the Church and its memory markers. Who else?"

He snorted a laugh. "I think you've been reading too many bargain-bin ebooks, my friend. Too many Clive Cussler and who's that new dude you've sunk your nighttime teeth into?"

"Steve Berry," Celeste answered.

"Yeah, I've heard he can spin a religious conspiracy yarn like it's nobody's business! Who would swipe those old bones anyhow, and during a wedding of all things?"

The group fell silent, cocking their heads and throwing him a knowing glare.

"Do I need to remind you, Hoss," Torres said, "about the last four years?"

He furrows his brow. "Oh, yeah. Suppose those pseudo-spiritual wackadoodle religious terrorists might want them bones."

Celeste turned to me, saying in a whispered rush, "You don't think this has the markings of Nous, do you, of your brother?"

I tightened my grip around the Glock. "Is it any question?"

Another rumble tore through the chapel—literally, the crack in the ceiling racing toward the altar now and brass candleholders rattling.

Glancing at Celeste, I nodded, my bride chambering a round in her own Glock and holding it like the sexy Charlie's Angels superhero she was—ready, willing, and able to face down the threat.

Man, did I love that look!

It was go time.

Again.

And on my wedding day!

At least I had my bride at my side.

Celeste said, "Naomi, would you be a good girl and help me with my dress?"

Torres raced to her back, working loose a few ties and hooks, then peeled away the larger, longer outer layer to her wedding dress, the pair setting it on the front pew.

"Right, shall we get on with it?"

Torres slid a small handgun from her inner thigh. "Locked and loaded."

"How come she's got a gun?" Gapinski complained.

"She came prepared," Celeste said. "Appears all the women have. And Eli."

Elijah stood tall, smiling with pride.

"Those exhibit cases," I explained, "are made from the strongest polycarbonate glass there is. Bullet proof and fireproof. Hopefully they earned their keep up top."

"Yeah, but bomb proof?" Gapinski questioned.

Another shudder put an exclamation point on Matt's question. Definitely wouldn't keep the hostiles out forever, and they'd already spent precious minutes chit-chatting about next steps.

"I'll keep everyone inside the chapel," Peter said.

"Jolly good, Pastor Young," Celeste said. "Secure the doors upon our exit and open them for no one. A deadlock at the latch should do the trick."

"Got it. But you better get to it. Grace and peace be with you all."

I nodded, readying my weapon. We'd need both in spades.

"Come on!" I shouted, racing down the aisle, our guests standing at attention and murmuring—whether from ceremonial respect or curiosity, it wasn't clear.

What was, was that we didn't have much time.

I came into a hallway, one leg racing toward a stairwell that ran to Order HQ guarded by nothing but a chain and Do Not Enter sign—something I'd have to fix when this was over—and the other leg running to a stairwell rising to the nave. Then spun around to instruct my comrades.

I jabbed a finger in Gapinski's chest. "You're with me." Then jutted my arm down the hallway to the right. "And we're going thataway. To the nave."

Jerking a thumb behind, I said to Celeste and Torres, "You two get to HQ and—"

"Bloody hell I will!" Celeste interrupted. "We're all going. Up to the top."

She leaned in with wide, insistent eyes. "*Together!*"

I'd heard something somewhere—probably my bachelor party, probably from Gapinski's virgin lips after a few shots of Grey Goose—some proverb ditty going like '*Happy wife, happy life.*'

The knot hadn't been tied just yet, but enough of the maxim had sunk into my lizard brain after too many shots of Grey Goose not to mess with the missus-to-be.

I snapped my mouth shut and promptly nodded.

Then jerked my head thataway and pounded through the limestone corridor.

Celeste close behind.

Not that I'd want it any other way. She and I had been joined to the hip on missions far more critical to the Church's survival—much less the world's—for the past four years. Ever since she'd saved my backside from getting a bullet planted square between the eyes. Which is funny, because the great saves from stories past were about the guy riding in on a white horse to save the day and rescuing the dame.

In my case, the dame rescued *me!*

Supposed the world has evolved a pinch since Sleeping Beauty.

The revving of an engine, joined by a *chunka-thunka-brrr* snapped me back to the moment, the four of us SEPIO agents pounding up the limestone stairwell in darkness, led only by the faint yellow LED emergency lights, emerging into the fading white light of the fading day up top.

And the smell of burning tires and diesel fuel and combustion and crushed stone, along with more of that grunting machinery and cries of danger—

Joined by the snapping of flaming fire!

"Silas..."

"I hear it," I replied. "I smell it..."

The narrow spiral stone staircase funneled us up to a doorway with its solid oak door unhinged and toppled. Just beyond the threshold was a completely unexpected sight.

Where century-old stone had been, browned with age and human wear, darkened by too few lights and brightened by baby blue tapestries edged by gold tassels, a gray light streamed through. It was interrupted by thickening storm clouds and some of that cut stone, but not in slabs of stacked limestone making up the walls to the narthex cathedral entrance. These were jagged, ragged monstrosities, bowing with injury and dressed with dancing wires sparking yellow and a few broken pipes spraying water.

"What the heck..." I muttered, pushing through the portal into the unknown world—the picture sharpening, the problem deepening.

The entire face of the National Cathedral had opened up into a wormhole out into the DC afternoon. Like a shotgun to the face, shredding a hole through a victim's head and leaving behind a wicked mess. Was any wonder the narthex hadn't collapsed.

Yet.

But how—

That *chunka-thunka-brrr* returned, yanking my attention stage right.

Where a massive excavator had clawed its way inside the nave!

Confusion seized the conscious part of my brain—confusion blooming how something like that could've happened. *Why* something like that could've happened! Lucky my lizard brain took over, the part that had been hammered and honed into automatic action by my ancestors battling saber-toothed tigers and fleeing mastodons before getting their tusks stuck up the tailpipe. Also had the advantage of Uncle Sam's memory muscle, all those years with the Rangers worth more than the stacks of Benjamins I'd gotten as compensation.

Which came in handy right about now.

Darting to the nave's entrance, not faring any better than the entryway, I could see what had gone down.

Must've barged through one of the entrance doors, the middle one decimated with the heavy oak door torn off its hinges and cast aside while the stonework was mauled and broken to bits. Then it barreled across the narthex straight inside the sacred worship space of the National Cathedral.

Why—now that was still the question.

"Holybamoly, Batman!" Gapinski complained. "It's like something out of a MCU feature film."

"MCU, Hoss?" Torres said.

"Yeah, Marvel Cinematic Universe. You know, like the Avengers and the Fantastic Four, Thor and Hulk and—"

"Matthew!" Celeste said, coming up next to me. "Neither the time nor the place."

"Sorry..."

"Suppose we know what all the rumbling was about," she said, surveying the damage.

Gapinski snorted. "Looks like someone with a Caterpillar had too much time on their hands!"

"Or a terrorist," Torres added, "hell bent on destroying America's church!"

"That sure takes the SEPIO cake. Haven't run into that one yet."

Celeste turned to me. "What do you make of it?"

I shook my head and went to answer, when movement caught my attention. From that damned excavator.

On instinct, I whipped out the Glock Elijah Fox had given me, training it on a black mass inside.

"Don't move, hands where I can see them!"

It was now that I saw the earth-mover beast had plowed right inside the nave reception area and right up to the Four Evangelists exhibit that stretched the threshold to the sanctuary.

Which lay in ruin! With cardboard displays shredded and cast aside, the polycarbonate cases cracked and smashed. First from detonation, as Torres had suggested. Then by the excavator's massive toothed scooper.

The *chunka-thunka-brrr* started up again—and the beast was moving, swinging its massive arm while raising its cupped hand lined with metal teeth.

Aiming straight for SEPIO.

No way, no how.

I opened up on the whack job, sending a volley of *pop-pop-pops* sailing into the cabin—joined by Celeste who had taken aim herself, our combined firing shattering the glass and killing the hostile.

"That'll do the trick," Gapinski said, hustling to the perp.

Torres added, "Definitely not what I expected when I slipped into my dress!"

She joined him, the pair confirming the hostile was dead as well as his identity. Celeste and I surveyed the excavator's damage.

Racing to the overturned cases, I searched the shattered

glass and wood—hoping, praying I'd find the relics amidst the rubble.

"Mind the jagged edges, love," Celeste said. "Would hate for you to lose a hand on our wedding day."

I threw her a wry grin. "Not a fan of one-handed husbands?"

"Might be, but let's get through the ceremony first. Then we can talk."

Frustration mounted the longer I searched. And fear. Because all that was leftover from the Caterpillar's rampage was the broken, busted cases and ruined displays.

And no bone relics.

All four Evangelists were missing.

Under my watch.

On my wedding day!

No use pissing and moaning about it. There was work to do. A mission to execute and an operation to launch headlong into.

On the double.

"And we've got a tat..." Gapinski announced.

I looked up at him climbing down from the, jaw clenched and gut tightening with disgust at the level my brother would sink to not only destroy the Church's memory markers born in these Four Evangelists. But also the lengths he would go to destroy me.

And Celeste...

Swallowing back the thought, I said, "Nous?"

He leapt from the rig and shook his head. "Nope. Different style. Some boxy cubist dude with some weird triangle head thingy."

"Theoti?" Celeste said, spinning toward him. "The Church of the Theotites operation conspiring with Nous?"

"Uh...yeah?"

I sighed, pressing my fingers against my temple and

rubbing. Supposed it was better than my brother, but still. Not what I needed, that's for sure, another religious whack job outfit threatening the faith.

On my wedding day!

I returned to the floor, rummaging through the rubble for the relics, but turned up empty.

Not good.

Only one thing that meant.

They were gone, the Theoti hostiles swiping them for Lord only knew what demonic design.

But with the one hostile still inside the excavator, him and his SEPIO crew having gotten the jump on him before he got away, maybe the others were still inside somewhere.

Also not good, because that meant a whole lot of friends and family were under threat.

"*Pst!*" someone sounded from behind.

Gapinski, pointing two fingers at his eyes, then throwing them deep into the nave darkened by those storm clouds rolling across the sky. He was crouching behind the excavator along with Torres, now waving a handgun out toward the pews dutifully lined across the stone floor for worship. Must've lifted it from the hostile.

But what he was getting at, I didn't—

The whispering clatter of rushing feet across stone caught my attention.

At the front crossing. Pairs of them. Along with two hunched figures darting for the shadows.

Two of them.

Something pinged in the back of my lizard brain. From earlier in the day. The three men I'd chatted with inquiring about the exhibition, who I hadn't recognized and assumed were part of Celeste's party.

Three men. These two scurrying in the shadows, plus the joker I'd just taken out inside the excavator.

Dammit...

They were right there, under my nose!

Although, suppose I did have other things on my mind.

Like getting married!

The two hostiles had the advantage of distance and the shadows, the storm clouds doing a number on the natural light dimming to nothing in the stained glass windows and the emergency lights doing nothing to help me and my team with any sort of visual deeper into the nave.

But from what I did see—we didn't have time to pussyfoot around the pew.

We need to get to it, take down the hostiles, and retrieve the stolen relics.

By force, if need be.

Clenching the borrowed Glock with one hand and taking aim, I motioned with my other hand for Celeste to take the far side of the nave with Torres as her backup and Gapinski as mine.

The women nodded and took off, Celeste taking point toward the north aisle with Gina Anderson's Glock, the two padding across the nave in their wedding getups quite the sight to see. Not that Gapinski and I were any different, the two of us edging along the far right south aisle in our penguin suits down toward the wood altar where I'd last seen—

The wall exploded above my head in a shower of stone.

"Sonofa—"

Dropping to the floor, I cut off Gapinski's curse with a *pop-pop-pop* rejoinder.

All shots going high and wide toward the front, the bullets sinking into the massive limestone columns as thick as sequoias and thudding off walnut wood stalls in the Great Choir.

Made me sick unleashing such menacing violence inside the sacred space, but it did the job. Sent the hostiles scurrying for cover which gave SEPIO the window it needed to hike it up the aisle.

Another *one-two-three* rounds echoed from behind the wood altar at the crossing, then another, this time aiming north and south—to me and Gapinski and at Torres and Celeste.

Which pissed me right off!

Knew my bride could more than handle herself. Would win a shoot-out at the OK Corral without thinking or blinking, hands down. Would beat my own backside at a shoot-out at the OK Corral without thinking or blinking!

But seeing her under fire like that—on our wedding day... boy, did it piss me right off.

So I tore down the aisle, my feet in those hard leather oxfords barking something fierce. Didn't care a lick. All that mattered was coming to Celeste's rescue!

Thankfully, all those years playing quarterback with the Falls Church Jaguars came in handy. Came up quick to a side baptistry—

Just as a tall, slender figure in black with wide shoulders and a duffle bag slung over his shoulder popped above the parapet of the massive wood table.

Slung a wicked-looking assault rifle from his side.

And took aim—

Lucky for me, I was quicker on the draw, letting loose a barrage of rounds that left a whole lot of brass casings tinkling to the stone floor with an echo that was only outmatched by the *pop-pop-pop-pop* explosion of gun fire.

All found their target, sinking into the Theoti's chest and one dead-center forehead. Had picked up that trick with the Rangers. Never knew when a hostile was wearing kevlar and would only be winded, not wounded—and terminally so.

Hence the stray shot to the kisser. Harder to make, given less surface area to aim for. But they don't say Rangers lead the way for nothing. Especially when it comes to felling religious whack jobs.

"That was easy," Gapinski snorted.

Approaching from the north, Torres corrected, "Don't press your Staples button just yet, *muchacho*…"

She padded to the other hostile, a *pop-pop* thrown up with a wicked echo. Guessing she went for the chest, and he was packing.

I quickly joined her, confirming a kill shot to the forehead.

"He was reaching for his weapon," Torres explained in defense. "Had no choice."

Gapinski scoffed. "But I shot him like four times in the chest!"

"The few, the proud…" I muttered, making a below-the-belt crack at his tenure with the marines. "You're right, Naomi, you didn't. Good work."

Huffing a sigh, I swept the nave and shoved the Glock at my back waist. What a desecration. Not only ruining my sacred day, my wedding day, which I was getting mighty tired of complaining about. But mostly for violating the worship space with violence and bloodshed.

The only redeeming part of it all was the black duffle bag lying between the two goons.

I knelt next to it and zipped it open.

Letting a breath I didn't know I was holding escape in frustration.

"Uh, chief, hate to break it to you," Gapinski said, craning over my shoulder, "but it looks like we're two fries short of a Four Gospels Happy Meal."

"A femur and mandible," Celeste added from across my other shoulder. "That's what appears to be missing."

"We've got a skull portion and finger bone," Torres said, "Matthew's and John's relics?"

I heaved a sigh, jaw clenched. "Which means Mark's and Luke's are MIA."

"Which also means our operation," Celeste said, raising her weapon and sweeping the nave, "is only half through."

"Always something..." Gapinski cursed.

"*Donde estan ellos?*" Torres asked.

Good question. Where are they indeed?

Things just got worse. Par for the SEPIO course.

"Right, you remain with these hostiles, Matthew," Celeste instructed, "whilst Naomi and I run farther aloft into the north transept. There are plenty of hiding places for our relics."

"And more hostiles..." I said, raising my own weapon and searching the vast space shrouded in shadows, thunder rumbling overhead now. "I'll head down the eastside. Couldn't have gotten far with the rest of the building locked for our ceremony."

Our ceremony...

I muttered a curse and shook my head. Par for the Silas course, is what this day has been.

"Jolly good," she said with a nod, then leaned in and pecked me on the cheek. "You be careful, you hear?"

"You as well."

She and Torres raced on, leaving me and Gapinski to get on with it.

He nodded toward a side chapel. "Go ahead, chief. They ain't goin' anywhere on my watch."

I nodded, thanking the man.

Then raced off after Mark's and Luke's relics, hoping they were still inside.

Two down, two to go. Supposed that counted for something.

Even if it was a relic heist on my wedding day!

Took not even eight steps when a wicked *rat-a-tat-tat* sliced through the nave.

"Hit the deck!" Gapinski yelled, bullets chewing through wood pews and sinking into limestone columns, sending stone splintering across my path.

The strafing bullets, no doubt from some Heckler & Koch automatic rifle, the weapon of choice for a certain nemesis—which sent me diving into the Children's Chapel and racing toward a slender, solid wood door.

Of course it was shut. Probably locked.

Which was pretty much par for the SEPIO course.

Was about the only option at this point.

Another livid set of relentless *rat-a-tat-tats* put an exclamation point on my current lot in life!

Leapfrogging over the back of the slender wood chairs, I landed with sure footing on the crimson padded seats and dashed down the small aisle to sail back to the stone floor.

Catching the edge wrong and stumbling overboard.

Caught most of the impact with my right shoulder, but pain bloomed from my right knee and lanced up my leg.

I was getting too old for this...

I choked back a curse and hobbled for the door, grasping the burnished bronze knob and giving it a twist.

Moment of truth...

Unlocked.

A first for SEPIO!

Which did my heart good, but also sent all sorts of administrative signals pinging my Master of the Order brain. Should've been locked, a stairwell winding down below, but glad it wasn't.

Wasn't responsible for the facilities, but was sure glad some janitor forgot to lockdown. A hefty bottle of Scotch whiskey with a big, red bow was in order for that blessed soul!

And a hefty raise.

Throwing opened the door, I dove inside and yanked it

closed—

Just as another menacing barrage of bullets thudded with a useless muffle into the other side.

Without a clue where Celeste was.

But I couldn't worry about that now. She was more than capable of taking care of herself.

Shoot. She'd taken care of the both of us in the exact kind of SEPIO operational scenario. The first one, in fact, saving me from no uncertain doom at the hand of that whack job Jacob Crowley half a decade ago.

So, no, I wouldn't worry about where she was or what she was doing. All that mattered was where the last two bone relics were.

And recovering them.

I scrambled from the floor and descended below, groping my way down the spiral stairs through the dark. Another door guarded the bottom, open and easing off the wall.

As if it had just been opened.

Adrenaline flooded my veins at the sight, the shadow beneath the door from the emergency light growing as the slab of wood kept easing shut.

I grasped its edge and eased it back open, a faint complaint squeaking with an echo that made me wince.

A long hallway stretched before me bathed in faint yellow light streaming from an emergency box planted above the door. Wood doors lined the limestone corridor, all shut, with a dark runner racing down the center. Smelled of stone and cleaning chemicals, with a faint salty tang of body.

Someone had definitely been through there. I could sense it, I could feel it.

Tightening my grip around the Glock, I padded down the corridor—discerning, intuiting, sensing the last remaining hostile.

Nothing but my own breath.

I kept going, on pace with my ticker galloping in my chest and pulsing alarms in my head.

From what I recalled, the hallway led under the High Altar, a bunch of administrative offices with salaries guaranteed by the endowment that stretched well into the eight figures. That's the Church for you. Employing ecclesial bureaucrats for the sake of it to raise more tithes to keep the engine humming. Suppose all bureaucracies were like that. My own included!

Had not a clue where I was going, but I kept going there anyway. Never got down to these parts of the Cathedral, the Order's headquarters several stories beneath and my own office sitting about right where I was now moving. Too much of my own bureaucratic bull to enjoy the spiritual fruits of my benefactor. I'd have to change that.

The shadows suddenly changed, the yellow-lit limestone opening up to a hallway racing west.

Eyes didn't even have time to adjust. It all ran together. Door, limestone, door, limestone, door, hallway—

And a bulky, hulking figure looming from the corner of my eye.

Now crashing into me and sending my Glock skittering across the floor.

Freakin' rookie mistake!

Before I could react, a massive palm pressed against my face and smashed my head against the wall. Then again.

A wicked *smack-smack* sounded, followed by a sharp tuning fork ting from the head trauma. Then a dimming darkness and sharp white starlight flashed, pain blooming and lancing through my head.

That'll leave a mark.

Couldn't worry about that now.

My face gripped firmly, the hostile wrenched my head back for round three when I smashed my fist into his jaw.

Heard his teeth knock together with a wicked clatter. Or I suppose her. Was certainly an egalitarian type when it came to my whack job hostiles getting the jump on me! The guttural moan escaping from behind those teeth told me my instincts were right the first time.

He staggered back, and I kept at it.

Rapped my closed fists together against the side of his head, throwing up another cry as the light caught his face just right.

Knew it. The Persian dude from the exhibit.

He staggered like a drunken sailor, a black duffle bag slipping from his shoulder behind.

The relic goods, I assumed.

"Figured I'd run into you at the reception," I said, bobbing and weaving with raised fists, "between the first course of potato leek soup and the main course of beef bourguignon."

He growled and came at me, sending a right hook sailing toward my face.

Which I blocked with both arms before ramming them into his own—a crack resounding from his nose and blood sputtering from his lips.

"An odd combo, I know," I went on, the man recovering and sinking a solid fist into my ribcage. I coughed and winced but returned the favor, skipping back a few feet and finding purchase farther down the hall in search of my Glock.

With the bad lighting and dark carpet, I wasn't having any luck.

"But we're catering from a French bistro I was at the last time you numbskulls reared your heads. Wanted a redo on their beef bourguignon from when my fiance and I were planning our wedding. Figured the big day was the day to do it."

A berserker scream echoed through the hallway, the man standing tall and puffing out his chest and spitting to the side before barreling toward me.

Must've gotten tired of my spiel.

Bringing my arms in tight, I braced for the impact.

It was severe.

Hard, solid muscle slammed into me. My stance absorbed much of the blow, and I followed up with a few well-placed punches, but it was no use.

Bending back, his arms exploded from him and connected squarely with my own unguarded chest—a split-second mistake I'd regret in no time flat.

The maneuver sent me sailing from my feet and landing hard on my back.

Head slammed against the floor with a wicked, cracking *smack!*—starlight and darkness threatening to take over.

It didn't, but I was spent—my breath snatched from me and waning adrenaline leaving behind moaning muscles and a screaming head.

Was a little surprised—and not a little ticked—I'd been defeated. But life as an ecclesial bureaucrat the past few years had softened this former Ranger.

I rolled over and went to my knees, then twisted around to face the man.

"This ends now!" he growled.

Yes, it does. Or not, Lord. Got a bone to throw?

"Just get it over with. I'm prepared to die."

"Are you now?" He was breathing hard. "For your pathetic religion? For these—what did you call them? Memory markers of the faith, these bones of those dead men who had spun stories of miracles and resurrection, teachings on love and peace and all such nonsense."

Heat raced up my neck and bloomed in my face a fiery crimson.

Mess with me and bring me to my knees—literally!—fine. I could take it.

Mess with my faith—my Savior and his story? Now, that

was a whole other ball of ugly!

Before I could do anything about it, the hostile closed his right eye and lined up his shot. Held it a beat before squeezing the trigger.

In that split second, my life flashed before my eyes. Cliché, I know, but all of what could have been, all of what *should* have been with me and Celeste, our family—anniversaries, dinners, birthdays, children, grand children, vacations—raced through me in a sour elixir that nearly sent me springing to my feet and charging the bastard!

But there flat wasn't time. I was out of it. Knew it to be true.

So, I gritted my teeth and held his stare, forcing the man to look me in the eyes.

Here we go...

Suddenly, the man lurched forward, the sound of three rounds echoing around the room.

I instinctively closed my eyes and snapped my head back, the aural explosion registering in my brain as an actual explosion to my forehead!

But I was still breathing—hard. Along with my pulsing heart pounding at full speed. And no pain, no warm, sticky blood flowing down my face or from my chest.

I opened my eyes and felt my chest.

Nothing.

Then sat up, checking myself over.

No blood, no wounds, no nothing.

The sound of the hostile's body slumping down and folding to the side caught my attention, his face twisting to one side. Blood was seeping from his mouth, and he was gasping for final breaths.

"No matter," he managed to cough. "What's done is done."

Wondered what his cryptic final words could mean. Then noticed that behind him stood Celeste, gun still outstretched.

She'd saved my life.

A second time!

Celeste stood still, feet spread apart with Torres at her side, eyes locking with mine.

"I had to," she said, as if trying to convince herself as much as me.

"I understand," I said, scrambling for her. "Absolutely."

"He was going to kill you." She lowered her gun and stood still, as if she didn't know what to do next.

"I know." I grabbed hold of her weapon, tugging it toward me and pulling her along with it.

We met in the middle. She met my eyes; I met hers. Our mutual adrenaline was magnetic.

Then one end of her mouth curled upward. "I do believe this is the second time in the past four years I've saved your ass."

I laughed. "We've gotta stop doing that."

"Good news, *muchachos*," Torres said, gesturing at the open duffle bag cast aside by the hostile.

Squinting in the faint light, I caught a glimpse of a pair of human bones.

Mark's and Luke's relics.

I sighed, then smiled. "It's over."

She smiled and nodded.

I threw my arms around Celeste, her shoulders slumping as the tension of the moment dissipated. She sank into me and I held her tight, not wanting to let go of her and wanting nothing more than to take her home—to *our* home.

Almost...

"Uh, guys!" someone's voice echoed toward us.

It was Gapinski, rushing in with eyes wide and heaving a desperate breath.

"What happened here?" he asked.

I said, "The hostile's dead. It's over."

Gapinski looked down at the body slumped on the floor,

then shook his head. "No, it's not."

My gut dropped to the stone floor. Of course not. Par for the SEPIO course.

As if reading my mind, Gapinski responded, "There's a bomb."

"Another one?" Celeste said.

I cursed under my breath, saying the quiet part out loud: "Of course things get worse—on my wedding day!"

He shrugged. "As they say, bad things come in pairs."

"It's threes. Bad things come in threes."

"Not sure that's any better, chief."

"Where is it, mate?" Celeste said, rushing to exit.

Gapinski jerked a thumb, then hesitated. "You're not gonna like it."

He was right.

Because after almost half a decade working for the Order, and the past few years as Order Master, I had gotten to know the National Cathedral pretty well. Especially a certain wing of its lower, subterranean level. And the route Gapinsk took us seemed to be winding its way toward—

"Are you bloomin' kidding?" Celeste exclaimed on our approach.

"Told you you weren't gonna like it," Gapinski muttered as we came to the chapel.

The one we had been inside when the whole thing started.

The one we were being married in when the whole thing started!

The room was still packed with guests, Pastor Young taking their command seriously to keep holed up inside the safe zone.

"This way!" Gapinski said, shoving inside the chapel. "Step aside, move!"

The crowd parted, us teammates following him to the front, at the altar—

Where Celeste and I and the others had been standing!

Celeste asked, "How the bloomin' blazes did you find a bomb?"

"I found it," Peter explained, "beneath the altar and behind the curtain after you left. The guests were getting restless, and I wondered if there was a pitcher of water underneath that I could use to make things easier on them. That's when I found—whatever it is, a bomb or whatever. Hadn't a clue, so I went for you folks and found Matt."

"Then I found you both," Gapinski added, "giving the hostiles the tap-tap-tappy to the back of the head."

"And you didn't think to clear the chapel?" Torres said.

"Didn't have time! Besides, I didn't know what we had, and with all the guests and roving religious terrorist whack jobs, I figured our first course was the best course."

"Well, let's get on with it," Celeste said. "Lead the way, Pastor Young."

Peter hustled to the ornate gold altar, parting a crimson velvet curtain. SEPIO gasped as one.

There it was.

A half bowling ball-size lump of combustible clay. Four pounds of that stuff could blow up a bus. There was at least double that stuck underneath.

And dead-center was a timer with red digits counting backwards.

It read 6:25.

Then 6:24.

Now 6:23.

"*Dios mío...*" Torres whispered.

"How the heck," Gapinski said, "did that thing get there?"

Celeste answered, "The hostiles must have planted it with all of the chaos of the day. Or perhaps after setup last night."

"Hope it wasn't an inside job..." he muttered.

None of it made sense. Especially that last part. Didn't

even want to think about that. Couldn't think about any of it, how it got there, why—who! All that mattered was defusing the bomb.

But—

My mind was a vortex of panic, all training and expertise from the military draining down a hole of fight-flight-freeze hyperarousal.

I'd left the military because of years of stress dealing with this stuff. Had even leveraged that training on my very first operation with SEPIO before I was a card-carrying member. Another bomb, left by Nous at the Church of the Holy Sepulcher to bury the spot of Jesus' burial—and resurrection.

Irony of ironies. Which wasn't lost on me in the slightest.

Now I was staring down the barrel of a red-digit timer threatening not only my life, but my livelihood!

And my future family.

Rage bloomed hot in my chest and raced to my face, the thought my brother, the head of that godless, wicked organization, had planned to blow me and Celeste up—

That blooming rage threatened to shut me down. I clenched my hands into a shaking fist, my jaw crushing my teeth with a fury I needed to fuel into action.

To save not only this church but these people.

My people!

First order of business: "Everybody out!"

I stood, sending my hands high into the air and motioning dramatically with a second call to evacuate—on the double.

They heeded my call, scrambling from their chairs and clattering in a rush out the door to get out of Dodge.

Hoped they had enough time, because the ticking clock was quickly winding down to zero.

With me on point to stop it.

"What do you make of it?" Celeste had crouched next to me as I stared at the bomb, frozen with indecision.

She waited a beat, then snapped her fingers. "Silas. Hello?"

I blinked, then looked at her blank-faced.

"You are the one to dismantle it. You did it before. What do we do?"

I fixed my eyes on the device again. Given my training with the Army as an Explosive Ordnance Disposal technician, a unique specialty alongside my training as a Ranger, I knew that most action movies and books got it wrong.

Most firing circuits, that is, the circuit in an electrically initiated explosive device, like the one staring me in the face, can be interrupted in literally any fashion to render the device "safe." Remove or cut any wire and you're good to go. None of this *which wire is the wrong wire*, nonsense. Firing circuits can be as complex or as simple as any other type of circuit.

Like the one counting down past 5:27.

Since the only other thing you need to complete the circuit is a power source, you can cut any wire in the circuit, thus breaking the circuit, and the device cannot work. There are still explosives present, and there are still measures that need to be taken for their safe removal, but the device will no longer function as designed. It's simple electronics, and the most common IED I'd encountered.

And yet...

I also knew that someone with a lot of electrical know-how could design a much better firing circuit. This is where the skill set of an EOD technician came into play.

Like me.

Or former training. Hadn't touched this stuff in almost twenty years! At least regularly. Last time was at that blasted chapel in the Church of the Holy Sepulcher in Jerusalem on my very first operation as an unofficial member of SEPIO.

Irony of ironies I was back in the saddle diffusing yet another bomb—right under my own roof.

And on my freakin' wedding day!

I sat staring at the device, diagnosing the circuit completely before taking any action.

Was this just a common simple circuit or a more complex collapsing circuit, the kind that cannot simply be interrupted at any point?

Someone could build a collapsing circuit in any number of ways, including using relays or semi-conductors, and various other electrical engineering techniques. Back in the Middle East, I'd seen all the possible ways to booby trap a circuit so that if a wire was cut, the device would still function.

Or worse.

The bottom line running through my head as I continued assessing the device was this: usually, any wire can be cut; sometimes it can't.

Which kind was this?

Another minute ticked by.

4:11 was quickly leading to 0:00.

"Talk to me, Silas," Celeste said gently, as if trying to prod me onward. "What are you thinking?"

"I'm thinking this could go one of two ways." I looked at her. "Either we succeed and dismantle it. Or we don't."

Torres snorted. "That's comforting..."

I ignored her, working out the possible outcomes depending on which wire I snipped and which wires I left unsnipped.

"Cutters," I muttered, mind snapping to work.

"What, love?" Celeste said.

"We need something to cut the wires."

"Can we just move it?" Gapinski asked.

"We could. C-4 is a pretty stable explosive compound, comparatively. But I don't know how it's rigged. That timer could have some sort of accelerometer triggering mechanism. We need to disable it as-is. Which means cutting one of the wires."

"Which means," Celeste added, "you need to disable it as-is by cutting one of the wires."

She nodded toward Gapinski, who raced out of the chapel for the goods.

Prayed he found them—and in time.

Waiting, I brought a hand up to my chin and twisted my head from right to left to examine the device.

Red, green, black, and grey.

Those were my options.

Red, green, black, and grey.

Red, green, black, and grey.

The colors and wires all ran together, and the proper procedure for diffusing them.

Gapinski returned in a lumbering rush, panting and sweating. But he had them, and he handed a pair of scissors over.

"Sorry, best I could do."

I snatched them and nodded, returning to the bomb. "They'll do."

Flipped the scissors around in one hand as I recalled the rhyme all first level EOD techs learned that would guide me to make the right decision.

"You're crazy in the head," I mumbled, "if you clip the red. Green means go, but not if there's grey. Don't play with grey no matter the day. Black means death; cut that one, you lose your breath. Live to see the light by cutting—"

I looked at Celeste, face blank with emotion.

"What is it?" she asked.

"There's no white wire!" I hissed.

I moved closer to the bomb, cranking my head from right to left, from top to bottom. Then I did it again.

Nothing but nothing.

"Live to see the light," I went on, swiping at a line of sweat trickling down my brow, "by cutting the white. That's the saying. Red, green, black, sometimes grey, and always white. There should be a white wire. But there's no white wire!"

I let slip a curse, then stood and raked a hand through my hair.

"What does that mean?" Celeste asked.

2:11.

2:10.

2:09.

Gapinski answered for me: "It means we're screwed. Sideways."

I ignored him, kneeling back down in a huff and shaking my head. Wiped away another bead of sweat winding down my right temple and cursed beneath my breath.

Then didn't: "Think, dammit!"

I thought about who I was dealing with, a Nous operative, or Theoti or whatever. Who surely knew what they were doing, and was part of an entity known for its interest in pyrotechnics, and certainly in violence. So a bomb matched the MO of these hostiles. But where there was any military or police experience with these jokers, and formal training...

That was the unknown.

And the variable that could make this whole thing spin on a dime.

And no white wire!

"Come on buddy," Gapinski said, "Less than a minute to go."

"I know, alright!"

0:59.

0:58.

At once I sat upright, resolve solidifying into decision.

It was a gamble. But it would go one of two ways. Yes or no. Life or death. Correct wire—

Or not.

I held the scissors in my right hand, then reached for the

grey wire.

I hesitated, the scissors sagging slightly.

0:40.

0:39.

"Silas," Celeste said.

I reached for the green wire and brought the scissors up to it, widening their mouth to sever the connection.

Then stopped short, retracting them back to my lap.

0:26.

0:25.

0:24.

"Love," Celeste said, "now would be the perfect time to show off those skills your always going on about Uncle Sam teaching you..."

I gave Celeste a searching glance. Waiting, intuiting, discerning what I should do next. After all, she'd been my right-hand gal in battle. Would be my right-hand gal till death us depart. So her say was golden in my book. Whatever say she had.

She looked straight into my eyes, then nodded. "Just do it."

I nodded back.

Then, raising the scissors up to the black wire, I held it steady and chopped through it—with one squeeze, then another. The wire gave.

But the count cycled down from 0:06 to 0:05.

Then to 0:04.

Then it stopped.

I held the gaze of the digital counter. And my breath.

Waiting, intuiting, praying to the good Lord above that it stayed stopped!

It did.

When I realized I was still alive and in one piece—that my wife-to-be and teammates were alive and in one piece—I sucked in a lungful of air, then slowly let it release.

"Yeah buddy!" Gapinski said, slapping my back.

Celeste laughed with relief. "Cracking good job, Silas."

I slumped to the floor, closing my eyes to center myself.

Peter and Torres offered the same congratulations. I was too wound up to acknowledge it.

Pounding footfalls outside the chapel drew my attention—and sent my gut sinking beneath the National Cathedral when they arrived.

Big-boned bruisers. All in black. Flashing all manner of acronyms—FBI, ATF, DCPD—along with rifles I'd flashed myself a time or twelve.

"*On the ground, on the ground!*" the men yelled in a cacophony that echoed where our vows should have been.

Then: "*Hands where we can see them!*" joined the same echoey cacophony.

"Don't have to tell me twice," Gapinski said, dropping to the stone floor and throwing up a squeaking, compliant complaint.

Celeste and I glanced at one another, shrugging and joining him, pancaking ourselves on the cold stone with arms and hands splayed out in front of us.

I sighed as a hulky agent mounted my back and wrenched my hands behind me, strong, stiff plastic ties cinched around my hands before I was violently yanked from the floor.

Things always get worse when SEPIO's involved.

And on my wedding day!

6:03 p.m.

Took a while, but our mistaken detainment was corrected when the authorities realized who we were. Not only Order

Master and SEPIO operatives, but the bride and groom and wedding party!

Several more hours passed for Metro PD and FD to do their things—the police department taking witness statements and marking evidence, not to mention clearing the building of any sign of anymore hostiles; the fire department cleaning up the mess in the nave and tending to the injured. Then several go arounds with the head of domestic terrorism with the FBI to convince them to let the show go on—our show, my and Celestes's.

Took some doing—and by doing, I mean *Celeste* doing her no-nonsense, driving ways at odds with her British sensibilities for politeness and deference—but thankfully the special agent in charge was an old friend. An old girlfriend, in fact, Brittany Armstrong. Had even joined them for an operation sussing out a demonic force rearing its head from America's near past. Now that was a trip and a half!

Was a bit miffed she wasn't invited to the wedding, but after DCPD swept the building, and Brit's own crew did their own Fed thing, she let all the guests back inside and gave us clearance to seal the deal. But only enough time to get hitched, then she'd take over the joint and have her investigative way with it.

So, we'd spent the last half hour corralling and cajoling a leary and weary group of friends and family into filing back down into the chapel. Thankfully, they did, our guests braving the horrific scene inside the nave to dip back down to the room that had almost become their tomb.

Before beginning, Pastor Peter brought Celeste and me together. "You two you're sure you're ready to—"

"Get on with it, Pastor Young!" Celeste interrupted, waving her bouquet. "I've waited my whole life for this day, and there will bloody well be hell to pay if I let a bunch of two-bit Nous hustlers ruin my wedding day!"

"Theoti," Gapinski corrected.

Which was the wrong move, and he instantly knew it!

Celeste threw him don't-even eyes before returning to Peter with the same.

"So, keep a stiff upper lip, hike up your knickers, and get us bloomin' married!"

Peter's eyes were wide, and he glanced my way.

I nodded. "What she said."

He smiled. "Alright then. Let's get this party restarted!"

"Jolly good, Peter. I knew I liked you the minute you were thrust headlong into one of our operations."

With all of our guests seated, and our groomsmen and bridesmaids all lined up and ready to go, Celeste and I clasped hands and faced Peter.

He grinned and put out his hands, motioning for us to face one another.

We did, our hands clasping one another in a never-letting-go grip; our gaze locking and never letting up.

"Now Silas repeat after me—" Peter began.

I took in a measured breath, pain lancing through my ribs from the melee but my near-marital bliss carrying me through.

"I, Silas, take you, Celeste, to be my wife," he said.

"I, Silas, take you, Celeste, to be my husband. I mean *wife*. I mean—what was the line again?"

The room erupted in laughter. Heat raced up the back of my neck with embarrassment. Although, it was a nice release valve after the super-heated afternoon of chaos.

"Let's try this again," Peter boomed over the echoey noise, eliciting another round of laughs. "I, Silas, take you, Celeste, to be my *wife*."

"Got it." Now I laughed, nodding. "I, Silas, take you, Celeste, to be my wife."

"And just remember, bro," Gapinski said. "Happy wife, happy life."

Another round of laughs, joined by clapping approval.

"Hear, hear, mate!" Celeste added.

I turned to him with a smirk. "Thanks. I'll keep that in mind."

"How about," Peter said, "we get back to the reason we're here: To get these two hitched. You know, before we're invaded by another group of terrorists!"

"Amen!" Gapinski shouted.

Peter searched his script, muttering, "Where was I…"

"The vows."

"Ah, yes. Here we go: I promise and covenant, before God and these witnesses…"

"I promise and covenant, before God and these witnesses," I repeated.

"To be your loving and faithful—" he paused, grinning "—*husband*."

Laughter rippled through the audience; I snorted along with them.

Then Celeste's eyes yanked me back to the moment, those pools of deep blue entrancing me in her love and snatching my breath.

I said, above a whisper, "To be your loving and faithful husband."

Peter went to continue, but I interrupted him, reciting the vows from memory now:

> *Sharing my life with you*
> *in plenty and in want*
> *in joy and in sorrow*
> *in sickness and in health*
> *to forgive and strengthen you*
> *to love and cherish you*

> *as long as we both shall live.*

Claps and whistles greeted my conclusion, along with some hoots and hollers from the Gapinski peanut gallery for good measure.

"Now, Celeste," Peter said, "repeat after me—with a little less drama this go around."

She giggled. "I should think not!"

I echoed her laughter, as did the room.

"I, Celeste, take you, Silas, to be my—" Peter glanced my way and winked "—*husband*."

Celeste giggled again, repeating: "I, Celeste, take you, Silas, to be my husband."

"I promise and covenant, before God and these witnesses—"

"I promise and covenant, before God and these witnesses..."

"To be your—"

"Loving and faithful wife," Celeste said with interruption, picking up the vows on her own and continuing on just as I had:

> *Sharing my life with you*
> *in plenty and in want*
> *in joy and in sorrow*
> *in sickness and in health*
> *to forgive and strengthen you*
> *to love and cherish you*
> *as long as we both shall live.*

Her face was beaming with the most elated look I'd ever seen on her—mouth wide and open, eyes bright and misting over. All of which was magical in and of itself, because that look was for me—because of me!

How did I get so lucky?

I matched her elation, my face hurting with so much joy and a surprising emotion rising from my throat to my eyes.

She squeezed my hands, and I squeezed back—three times, our silent code.

I. Love. You!

Her smile widened into a grin, those beaming eyes of hers spilling over, tears sliding over those perfect cheekbones of hers. On cue, she squeezed my hands the hardest she'd squeezed before:

I. Love. You. Tooooo!!!

My head swam with tingly disbelief at the shared moment, my chest warmed and overflowed with the purest emotion I'd ever felt. The emotion of heaven itself. Of love!

"Now, let's have those rings," Peter announced.

Letting go, and batting at the emotion that had taken over my own eyes, I turned toward Gapinski.

Who was half falling asleep!

"Matt," I whispered.

Nothing but a head nod and droopy eyes. Then a stagger before a snort back to the land of the living.

"Hey!" Torres shouted. "Get with the program, Hoss!"

His eyes flashed wide, and he glanced around—clearly seeing all eyes on him.

He pointed to himself, mouthing *Me?*

"The rings!" I whispered.

Gapinski stiffened and nodded, swallowing hard before fishing inside his jacket pocket.

Those eyes of his flashed wide again. He offered a smiley giggle before rushing for his side pants pockets.

Right.

Then left.

Nothing.

A sweaty sheen glistened across the man's face, crimson rising—along with my anxiety!

He switched to his coat pockets.

Right. Left.

Nothing but more nothing!

"Stuff and nonsense..." Celeste muttered.

"Got'em!" Gapinski exclaimed, yanking his hand from his back pocket. He handed them over, huffing a sighing breath.

"Right where I left 'em, and I left 'em right where I—well... erm left 'em. For me to find, I mean. Or...something."

I smiled, patting his arm. "Thanks, brother."

Snatching them, I handed them off to Peter. The reverend opened the boxes and withdrew the rings, their pure white gold glinting in the candlelight, and held them high.

Clearing his throat, Peter explained. "These rings are far more than just jewelry. They're symbols. Symbols for this marriage. First, note they are made from precious metal, reminding us of the sacredness of marriage. They're also infinitely circular, symbolizing the unity between a man and a woman becoming one. Finally, they are boundary markers, telling the world you belong to each other and no one else."

Handing off Celeste's ring, he said, "Silas take this ring—"

I took it, the massive diamond anchored at the center glistering all the colors of the rainbow, holding it carefully by four fingers. Two indexes, two thumbs.

Wasn't letting that puppy out of my sight again after Gapinski's near mishap!

"—and repeat after me," Peter continued. With each line, I voiced what that precious symbol meant to me.

"Celeste, I love you and I give you this ring as a symbol of my love and faithfulness; and with all that I am and all that I have—I honor you."

Then I slipped it on her tanned ring finger. Like Cinderella's glass slipper, it was. A perfect fit!

She grinned, an elated giggle slipping from her lips. Would never get old as long as I lived.

"Celeste, take this ring—" Peter said, handing off my own white gold band etched by a tiny bead pattern "—and repeat after me."

She did, voicing what I myself had voiced: "Silas, I love you and I give you this ring as a symbol of my love and faithfulness; and with all that I am and all that I have—I honor you."

I grabbed both of her hands again, ready to get down to business.

Our marriage business!

Turning toward the audience, Peter grabbed my arm. "Not so fast, killer. You're not married yet!"

"We're not?" I said, the room erupting in laughter.

"Almost, but not quite." He gestured off-stage to a pair of lit candles dutifully waiting their turn, once-long sticks of pale wax nearly stubs now after the afternoon of chaos, and a single, long unlit candle at the center.

The unity candle.

The organ struck up its bellowing pronouncement again, the same tune that brought us together at the start. Pachelbel's "Canon in D."

Taking a breath, I nodded, guiding Celeste toward the last leg of our wedding journey—and quite the journey it had been!

There was barely anything for us to grab hold of, but we managed, each of us wrenching loose our candle from its spent wax and guiding it as one toward the center—lighting the one candle.

The words of Mark's Gospel, something Jesus had said about the sacred nature of marriage, flashed into my mind, and I had an idea. Wasn't planned, but given what had happened earlier, it seemed appropriate. No way in hell would I let this candle snuff out after all we'd been through!

I quoted them then and there: "At the beginning of creation God 'made them male and female. For this reason a man will leave his father and mother and be united to his wife, and the two will become one flesh.' So they are no longer two, but one flesh. Therefore what God has joined together, let no one separate."

"Amen," Celeste said, joined by a smattering of others.

"Amen," I said, smiling at Celeste before grabbing her hand and guiding us back.

"Now are we hitched?" I said with a chuckle.

"Almost," Peter said with a smile. "Given our afternoon ordeal, why don't I pray over your new lives together."

"Yes, please!" we both said in agreement, laughing, the room joining in.

Raising his hands above us, Peter prayed, "Most gracious God, we give you thanks for your tender love in sending Jesus Christ to come among us, to be born of a human mother, and to make the way of the cross to be the way of Life. We thank you, also, for consecrating the union of Silas and Celeste in his name."

Taking a breath, he continued, "Now, by the power of your Holy Spirit, pour out the abundance of your blessing upon Silas and Celeste: defend them from every enemy; lead them into all peace; let their love for each other be a seal upon their hearts, a mantle about their shoulders, and a crown upon their foreheads."

I nodded. Wanted nothing more from the Lord for us and our new lives together.

"Send your blessing, O God, upon these your servants, that they may so love, honor, and cherish each other in faithfulness and patience, in wisdom and true godliness, that their home may be a haven of blessing and peace; through Jesus Christ our Lord, who lives and reigns with you and the Holy Spirit, one God, now and forever. Amen."

"Amen," the room echoed.

"Amen," Celeste said.

"Amen," I agreed, crossing myself.

Gapinski grasped my shoulder. "I think the moment you've been waiting for all day is finally here, chief."

"Thank the good Lord above!" I said.

"Agreed!" Celeste said with a nod.

Peter laughed, saying, "Now, Silas and Celeste, by the authority given to me as a minister of the Church of Jesus Christ and District of Columbia, it is my joy and honor to pronounce you husband and wife. Silas, you may now kiss your lovely new bride!"

"Finally!" I exclaimed. "Come here, darling."

She grinned. "Gladly..."

Without waiting a second more—

Celeste grabbed a fistful of my ruffled tux shirt and yanked me toward herself, pressing those luscious English-bred lips of hers against mine, sending a bolting jolt of euphoria skating through me.

What a surprise that was!

A welcomed surprise.

Went so fast I forgot to take a breath, but she gave me some of hers, our mouths connecting in a way they hadn't before. Even slipped some tongue in for good measure. Figured we'd both deserved it after what we'd just gone through.

Celeste agreed, returning the favor.

Time hung between our lips, our passion, our—

"Alright, alright. Get a room!" Gapinski complained from behind. "For Pete's sake..."

The chapel erupted in applause. Whether it was for our performance or Gapinski's insistence, it wasn't clear.

Another second slipped by before we released and caught our breath.

We opened our eyes at the same time, the same stumbling-drunk grin playing across our faces.

"Now that was positively magical, Master Grey," Celeste whisperer.

I leaned in, whispering back, "There's more where that came from, *Mrs.* Grey."

She hummed with pleasure. "I like the sound of *that*!"

"Which part? About their being more or about you being a missus?"

"Both." Her grin matched my own before giving me another peck.

Another taste, really, of what was to come.

For the rest of our lives.

"Ladies and Gentleman," Peter boomed above the continued clapping fray, "it is my privilege to present to you Mr. and Mrs. Silas and Celeste Grey."

The applause grew into a crescendo of whistles and hoots and hollers.

Celeste and I—

Wait, correction: my wife and I dashed down the aisle, then made for a set of stone stairs leading back to the still-smoldering surface. Then made for a cherry red Corvette convertible I'd rented for the afternoon that was now cresting toward evening—lunch plans ruined and our wedding nearly derailed.

Didn't matter, not one lick.

Because we climbed inside and peeled out of that circular drive faster than our friends and family could catch us, fingers wound tight around one another and hearts melded together as one—literally driving off into an inflamed sunset.

And into the rest of our lives.

Together.

Till death us depart.

ENJOY THE ADVENTURE?

A big thanks for joining Silas Grey and the rest of SEPIO on their adventure saving the Church! **Here's what's next:**

If you're ready for another adventure, you can get a full-length novel in the series for free! Join the insider's group to be notified of specials and new releases by going to this link: www.jabouma.com/free

SOLVE A GROUP X CASE!

Join the newest editions to the Order of Thaddeus, Elijah Fox and Gina Anderson, as they solve supernatural suspense mysteries for the investigative agency Group X. www.groupxcases.com

Read *Not of This World* today: bouma.us/gx1

GET YOUR FREE THRILLER

Building a relationship with my readers is a joy of writing! Join my insider group for updates, giveaways, and your free novel—a full-length, action-adventure conspiracy mystery in my *Order of Thaddeus* thriller series.

Just tell me where to send it. Follow this link to subscribe: www.jabouma.com/free

ALSO BY J. A. BOUMA

Nobody should have to read bad religious fiction—whether it's cheesy plots with pat answers or misrepresentations of the Christian faith and the Bible. So J. A. Bouma tells compelling, propulsive stories that thrill as much as inspire, offering a dose of insight along the way.

Order of Thaddeus Action-Adventure Thriller Series

Holy Shroud • Book 1

The Thirteenth Apostle • Book 2

Hidden Covenant • Book 3

American God • Book 4

Grail of Power • Book 5

Templars Rising • Book 6

Rite of Darkness • Book 7

Gospel Zero • Book 8

The Emperor's Code • Book 9

Deadly Hope • Book 10

Fallen Ones • Book 11

The Eden Legacy • Book 12

Silas Grey Collection 1 (Books 1-3)

Silas Grey Collection 2 (Books 4-6)

Silas Grey Collection 3 (Books 7-9)

Backstories: Short Story Collection 1

Martyrs Bones: Short Story Collection 2

Group X Cases Supernatural Suspense Series

Not of This World • Book 1

The Darkest Valley • Book 2

Against These Powers • Book 3

Luck Be the Ladies • Novelette

End Times Chronicles Sci-Fi Apocalyptic Series

Apostasy Rising / Season 1, Episode 1

Apostasy Rising / Season 1, Episode 2

Apostasy Rising / Season 1, Episode 3

Apostasy Rising / Season 1, Episode 4

Apocalypse Rising / Season 2, Episode 1

Apocalypse Rising / Season 2, Episode 2

Apocalypse Rising / Season 2, Episode 3

Apocalypse Rising / Season 2, Episode 4

Antichrist Rising / Season 3, Episode 1 (May 2023)

Antichrist Rising / Season 3, Episode 2 (June 2023)

Antichrist Rising / Season 3, Episode 3 (July 2023)

Antichrist Rising / Season 3, Episode 4 (August 2023)

Faith Reimagined Spiritual Coming-of-Age Series

A Reimagined Faith • Book 1

A Rediscovered Faith • Book 2

ABOUT THE AUTHOR

J. A. Bouma believes nobody should have to read bad religious fiction—whether it's cheesy plots with pat answers or misrepresentations of the Christian faith and the Bible. So he tells compelling, propulsive stories that thrill as much as inspire, while offering a dose of insight along the way.

As a former congressional staffer and pastor, and award-nominated bestselling author of over forty religious fiction and nonfiction books, he blends a love for ideas and adventure, exploration and discovery, thrill and thought. With graduate degrees in Christian thought and the Bible, and armed with a voracious appetite for most mainstream genres, he tells stories you'll read with abandon and recommend with pride—exploring the tension of faith and doubt, spirituality and culture, belief and practice, and the gritty drama that is our collective pilgrim story.

When not putting fingers to keyboard, he loves vintage jazz vinyl, a glass of Malbec, and an epic read—preferably together. He lives in Grand Rapids with his wife, two kiddos, and rambunctious boxer-pug-terrier.

www.jabouma.com • jeremy@jabouma.com

www.ingramcontent.com/pod-product-compliance
Lightning Source LLC
Chambersburg PA
CBHW070519200726
48293CB00007B/2595